Taking a Chance

A Professor-Student, Age Gap, Second Chance Romance

Rosie Darden

Red Zone Publishing

Contents

Prologue

TYLER

"You've done a surprisingly good job here, Tyler," the dean remarked, as he stood in the doorway of my office. "I'm glad we took a chance on you."

Not sure what was so surprising, but I knew better than to be snarky to my boss. Getting this position at the college was one of the highlights of my life. It was down to me and another guy, some Ive Leaguer who had ties to the Biology professor here.

"Thank you..."

"Have a great night, Tyler."

"You too, sir," I said as I began to pack up my bag. I needed to grade papers, but could do that over a plate of spaghetti carbonara from the comfort of my own home.

"So, question for you. Are you the *best* Literature professor here, Professor Stone?" a peppy voice said from the doorway.

"Depends on who is asking, I suppose." I counter, looking into the most beautiful brown eyes I've ever seen.

"What can I do for you Tiffany? What literary conundrum brings you in?"

"Well, I was pondering the deeper meaning of the symbolism in 'The Great Gatsby,' and I thought, who better to ask than the professor who knows all the secrets?"

"Ah, 'The Great Gatsby,' a literary masterpiece indeed. The green light at the end of Daisy's dock, you see, symbolizes..."

We continued a spirited discussion of literary motifs and themes, our words flowing like a well-rehearsed symphony. In that moment, it was clear that Tiffany's passion for literature was not only infectious but also irresistibly charming. And I couldn't help but notice how her brunette hair rolled down her shoulders, and her skin clearly saw plenty of sun; she was a nice golden tan which brought out the sparkle in her brown eyes. She was petite and lean, in kelly green pants and a white cotton top with embroidered flowers.

As much as I was accustomed to speaking, my mouth would intermittently go dry at the sight of her standing in front of me, listening to me intently. This was a new experience for me.

No one like *this* though. Maybe because she was standing so close to me. It was utterly unnerving and I couldn't look away long enough to quell the affect she was having on my stomach. What *is* this? I'd noticed Tiffany in my class, but having her in my office in a private conversation was completely different. Her affect on me was shocking. I felt drawn to her in a way I couldn't describe. It was magnetic.

"Right, well, I'll be ready for the exam now I think, Professor Stone."

"Yes, I think you'll do great, Tiffany!" I said in as an encouraging tone as possible, head nodding and a grin plastered permanently on my face.

She laughed, and I couldn't help but smile as I watched her. Her brown sparkling eyes looked into mine, and it felt like I was being swept away into a tunnel, where she was the only thing I could see there at the end of everything.

As Tiffany turned to leave, I couldn't resist the urge to continue our conversation, so I asked, "Do you come from around here, Tiffany? I haven't seen you before this semester."

She paused and turned back with a soft smile. "Actually, I'm from Yellow Point. It's a small town not too far from here. I just transferred to this college."

"Yellow Point, huh?" I replied, intrigued. "I've heard it's a beautiful place. How's the transition been for you?"

"It's been... interesting," Tiffany admitted, leaning against the doorframe. "I miss my best friend, June, we've known each other since high school. But I've always been fascinated by literature, so being here in your class, it's kind of a dream come true."

Her honesty was refreshing, and I found myself drawn into the conversation. "That's great to hear. And I must say, your insights in class have been quite impressive."

She blushed slightly, a mix of modesty and pleasure evident in her expression. "Thank you, Professor Stone. The characters really come to life in my imagination. It's like unraveling a mystery, isn't it?"

Our conversation meandered from literature to life in Yellow Point. She mentioned her struggles with asthma, which had shaped much of her childhood. This revelation added a layer of resilience to her character that I found admirable.

"Sounds like you've had to be quite strong," I commented, genuinely impressed.

Tiffany shrugged modestly. "I guess it's just a part of who I am. It's taught me to appreciate the little things in life, like a good book or a deep conversation."

I couldn't help but smile at her response. "Well, I'm glad it brought you here, to my class."

She laughed, a light, melodic sound that filled my office. "Me too, Professor Stone."

As she turned to leave again, I found myself saying, "If you ever need any help or just want to discuss literature, my door is always open, Tiffany."

She glanced back, her eyes bright with an unspoken understanding. "Thanks, Professor Stone. I might just take you up on that."

And with that, she left, leaving a lingering sense of connection that I hadn't felt in a long time. Her presence had brought a new energy into my life, one that was both exhilarating and slightly unsettling. As I sat back in my chair, I couldn't help but wonder about the journey that lay ahead.

·♥·♥·♥·♥·♥·

As the semester progressed, our connection deepened, weaving through our academic interactions and subtly permeating into personal lives. Our conversations often lingered after class, meandering from literary analysis to personal anecdotes. Tiffany's stories about Yellow Point painted a picture of a close-knit community, her words tinged with nostalgia and affection.

One late afternoon, as the autumn sun cast a golden hue through my office window, Tiffany stopped by to discuss an upcoming assignment as I was in the midst of tidying up my office, preparing to call it a day. Looking up, I see her standing there, her breaths slightly labored, and a hint of discomfort in her eyes.

"Tiffany," I said, "are you alright?"

She offered a tentative smile, which didn't quite mask the strain in her breathing. "Just a bit out of breath, Professor Stone. My asthma decided to make an unscheduled appearance today."

My heart went out to her. I'd known about Tiffany's struggles with asthma, but this was the first time I had witnessed it firsthand.

"Please," I gestured for her to come in and take a seat, "take your time."

Tiffany reached into her bag and retrieved her inhaler. As she took a deep breath and administered the medication, I watched with empathy, realizing that, in that moment, my office was a sanctuary for her, a place where she could catch her breath both literally and figuratively.

As the inhaler did its job and her breathing gradually eased, I couldn't help but admire her resilience. Tiffany had faced challenges that many others hadn't, and yet she continued to push forward with determination. It was a reminder that strength came in many forms, and Tiffany possessed it in abundance.

Once her breathing had steadied, Tiffany looked up at me with a grateful expression. "Thank you, Professor Stone."

I offered a reassuring smile. "Of course, Tiffany. No unwelcome visitors are allowed in here."

In that moment, as I watched her regain her composure, I felt a deeper connection forming between us. It wasn't just about being her professor; it was about under-standing and supporting her in every way I could, even when it meant providing a safe space for something as simple as catching her breath.

"Sorry about this, Professor Stone. I came to thank you, not turn your office into a treatment room. It's just an on-going saga in my life." Tiffany confessed, a hint of vulnerability in her voice. I listened intently as she spoke of her high school years, her friendship with June, and the challenges of managing her asthma. She described how literature had been her refuge, a world where she could breathe freely and find solace. There was a pause, a moment suspended in time.

"Now that the semester is about to finish, I guess this is where we say goodbye, and I just wanted you to know how much my time spent with you, um in your class, has meant to me" she said softly, a hint of sadness in her eyes.

I nodded, the weight of our situation heavy on my shoulders. I dreaded the end of our sweet explorations into literature, into life and all that makes it whole. "As your professor, this is where our path diverges. But as someone who has grown to respect and admire you, it's hard to just say goodbye."

Tiffany looked up, her expression a mix of hope and uncertainty. "Maybe this isn't the end, then? Maybe it's just a new beginning, in a different way?"

Her words echoed in my mind, a tantalizing possibility. Yet, the reality of our situation was inescapable. We were bound by societal norms and professional ethics, a boundary that couldn't just be blatantly ignored, not if I wanted to continue teaching. The rules of the college were quite clear on dating students.

"As much as I want to explore what this could be, we need to be mindful of the consequences," I said, the words tasting bittersweet. We locked eyes and I swear we were momentarily connected at a deeper soul level. I could feel her thoughts, her emotions, her very essence as our gaze drew out longer and longer.

Tiffany nodded, a silent understanding passing between us. "I know. But no matter what, this semester has changed me. You've changed me. Honestly right now, it feels a bit like Gatsby and Daisy – just an unattainable possibility."

"Well, yes but I hope I don't end up dying at the end of our story like Gatsby! You've changed me too, Tiffany. You've reminded me of the passion that drove me to teaching in the first place. Your curiosity, your zest for life, it's been inspiring."

We stood there, in the quiet of my office, a myriad of emotions swirling around us. It was a farewell, yet if I tried hard enough, I could sense the feeling that it actually *could* the beginning of something – something undefined, a story not forever paused at a crucial juncture.

I stuck out my hand awkwardly, desperate to touch this woman, to hold her in my grasp if only for a fleeting moment. I hoped the touch of her hand would burn into me, marking me forever. Instead, she took my hand as an invitation, and moved her other hand behind me in an unexpected embrace. God, it felt good to have her in my arms. I ran my hand along her back, and as I stepped back, my hand lingered at her waist a fraction of a second too long.

She hugged me tighter, willing the moment to last. As I forced myself to take a step back, or at least consider it, our faces close were within inches, centimeters of each other. I breathed her in and decided in that split second that my willpower may not be strong enough after all. She was clearly attracted to me as much as I was her. Tentatively, I brushed her lips with mine. She tilted her head up even more, lips parting and eyes closing as she leaned into the kiss. It was soft and tentative at first, a gentle exploration that quickly deepened. Our breaths mingled, hearts racing in unison. The world around us faded into a blur, leaving only the electric connection between us. Her hands moved up to cradle my face, fingers weaving through my hair, as the kiss grew more passionate. In that moment, all doubts and hesitations melted away, and I knew that this was where I was meant to be – lost in the embrace of a moment that felt as inevitable as it was unexpected.

"Tiffany, this is fantastic but it could cost me my job. It's a risk I just can not entertain right now. I'm so sorry." Her face fell.

"I do understand, Professor Stone. But it sure is a shame."

As Tiffany left my office that evening, I was left to reflect on the past few months in the solitude of my office. Tiffany had entered my life as a bright student, but she had become so much more. She had become a symbol of possibility, a reminder of the unpredictable paths that life can take. But what choice did I have?

I couldn't just end my career for a possibility of love with a student, one who was much younger and not fully developed into the person she would eventually be.

CHAPTER ONE

Games

TIFFANY

"Aren't you lonely in that house since he left?"

"For the hundredth time... He didn't leave. I broke up with him and asked him to move out," I reply, trying as hard as I can not to roll my eyes.

Mrs. Paulson is one of the customers that comes into the toy store at least twice a week with her two boys, ages 5 and 7, and I need to keep her business. But she is grinding my gears more than ever. *Slow, deep breaths, Tiffany*, I tell myself, mentally checking the locations of my inhalers. I always kept one in my purse and another behind the counter in a drawer. My asthma was largely under control, but I needed to manage my stress still and it was comforting to know I had inhalers available if needed.

"Mhm... Sure, sure thing, honey. Whatever you need to tell yourself," she replies and gives me an odd look as if she doesn't believe that I am the one who left Brian and not the other way round.

"Mrs. Paulson, I ended the relationship. Why is that so hard to believe?"

"Oh, it's not... it's not!" she exclaims but it's more than obvious that she's just saying what she thinks I want to hear.

The woman meanders through the toy store like she usually does, looking around until the kids locate a toy or two that they will break later. Which will cause her to come in again. I am grateful for a moment in which I can tend to some of the other customers but she's not about to let me off the hook that easily.

"So... how is Brian doing these days?" she asks while examining her long, sharp, red nails.

"I don't know, Mrs. Paulson. I'm not in contact with him anymore. As you can imagine, he's not exactly my favorite person after what happened. Can I get you anything else? Or have you decided on just the Captain America plushie?" I try to steer the conversation away.

The boys emerge from the side room of the toy store. Their arms are full of toys which they unceremoniously drop onto the counter by the check out register.

"Well, I saw Brian a couple of days ago at Jake's," she carefully says, relishing every word. Of course she did. Jake's is everyone's favorite restaurant in Yellow Point, and I'm sure it's responsible for hosting many of the town's key decisions, over freshly baked brioche bread which made the most delicious sandwiches. But why is she prattling on about seeing my ex there? Sometimes I get the feeling that she comes in here just to taunt me.

"I really don't care, Mrs. Paulson..." I say flatly. I might actually believe myself at this point. Brian was so much fun in the beginning, but fun turned to just immaturity when it was time to well, *adult* a bit. Brian seemed forever stuck in not-quite-a-full-fledged-adult stage.

Her face flushes a bit as she is not expecting this answer from me. No doubt the achingly bored woman has nothing better to do in the middle of the day than to spend long moments with two unruly boys in aisles and aisles of toys and games, in a bid to find fulfillment within the cellophane packaging of one or more of the boxes they grab. Which toy will entertain for hours and provide the peace she seeks? I know this is the real reason she comes in so often. Today, her boredom is demanding immediate attention, and I am unwittingly her muse. She wants me to get angry and take the bait. I do not.

"Well, maybe you will care when I tell you that I saw him with... her."

"Her? Her who? Cher?" I make a lame attempt at a joke.

She looks at me with a blank face, the joke clearly missing her completely.

"I saw Brian with Crystal. His girlfriend..." Mrs. Paulson replies and puts a lot of emphasis on this last word, trying to get some type of reaction out of me. That would make her day and she would, no doubt, have something to talk about later with her friends.

I turn around and look for a bag in which to deposit all the new toys she is buying. The bags are right there on the counter, but I need to get away from her for a second. When she notices that I still don't have a reaction to her news, Mrs. Paulson tries to turn the knife one more time.

"Come on, Tiffany! You know Crystal... Didn't Brian and Crystal... date while..." she says.

"They didn't date. Brian cheated on me with her, Mrs. Paulson," I cave and reply. "I would hardly call that dating."

The woman grins and taps her long, red fingernails on the counter.

"Huh... Is that so?" she asks even though she knows very well that's what happened. Sometimes it feels like the entire town knows what you ate for breakfast, let alone an interesting piece of information such as the boyfriend of the toy store manager cheating on her with a waitress.

But Mrs. Paulson's boredom is ravenous today, and she needs something to pull her out of her own routine.

"You know what you should have done, Honey?" she says, changing her tone now.

"Mrs. Paulson, the boys... They're riding the wooden horses in the window display. The horses are vintage – over a hundred years old!"

She turns and watches her children going bananas on my vintage wooden horses. Instead of reprimanding them, Mrs. Paulson waves a manicured hand in the air and returns to the far juicer conversation she believes we are having.

I emerge from behind the counter and playfully encourage her children off the horses with little luck. Another woman in the store watches but says nothing.

"So, let me give you a piece of advice," Mrs. Paulson says reassuringly as if this is her own talk show on daytime television.

"Great, could you give me a piece of advice on what to do about your boys?" I say but she pays no attention.

"They won't hurt anything. Tiffany, you should have cheated on Brian right back!" she announces as if she's just discovered plutonium.

"That's a... fantastic idea, Mrs. Paulson..." I reply with as much sarcasm as I can keep under control.

"No, really! Think about it, Tiffany. That would have shown him – he'd know exactly how it feels to have your heart ripped in two!"

"You know, I don't think it would have fixed anything, Mrs. Paulson. Brian didn't care about me to begin with since he slept with some random...*person*, even though we had been in a relationship. I honestly don't think that me sleeping with someone else would have mattered to him," I reply and get back behind the counter to serve someone else.

Mrs. Paulson's children are now kicking the wooden horses. Every little kick is a punch to my heart.

"Anywho, you still should have done it!" she replies, and her misuse of grammar is like nails on a chalkboard to my ears. "Are you dating anyone now?"

Anxious to end all of it – the inane conversation, the chaos being laid upon my sweet vintage horses, the noise – I respond with only a curt "Mrs. Paulson, are you ready?"

"What do you mean, Hon?"

"Will you be making any further purchases, or is this it?"

"Oh, I just like to let the kids decide. You know that already though, right? We come in to see you every other day! Now... what was I saying?"

I groan to myself and turn around, starting to dust a shelf and the toys on it. The only other person left in the store now is the older lady who is likely looking for a birthday present for her grandson.

"Can I help you with something, Miss Betty?"

"Oh, no, dear. I'm just... browsing, as they say..." she smiles.

Mrs. Paulson corners me again before I have the chance to disappear in the back.

"So, do you think you'll take up dating again soon, Tiffany? You're a... pretty decent looking girl," she asks scanning me from head to toe.

"Umm... thanks, I guess. Yeah so I don't think that we need to be talking about my dating plans."

"Come on! What's wrong with a little girl talk? Tell me! Are you still in love with Brian? Is that what it is?" she asks as she leans in over the glass counter. Her cheap perfume smells like peaches and plastic.

"No, Mrs. Paulson, of course not. In fact, I'm happy that I got to see who Brian is before our relationship progressed."

"Progressed?"

"Before we got married. In a weird way, I suppose I'm thankful that he cheated on me now. It's much easier to end a relationship than a marriage. Now I can pick up the pieces and figure out what I truly want from a man."

"Huh..." she looks at me with her mouth slightly open as if this is the first time someone has flown these ideas her way. "And... is that why you're waiting to date?"

"In part, I suppose. I don't want to rush into anything. Not to mention that I don't want to go through the same experience I went through with Brian."

"How will you avoid that...?" Mrs. Paulson asks.

"Well... Brian was somehow more immature than I thought, and not ready for a committed relationship. He cheated on me, disrespected me, and didn't care at all about hurting me. I don't want that to happen again. The next time I decide to commit my heart to someone or, even better, to accept dating in the first place, I want to know that he is mature, confident, that he knows what he wants and, most of all, that he won't be so careless with my heart," I explain as I get lost in my own musings.

Mrs. Paulson is now staring at me with a blank expression on her face, clearly taken aback by the serious tone of the conversation. This is not what she had in mind when she came into the toy shop and started antagonizing me.

"Where are you going to find a man like that?" she asks.

Before I can answer, the boys walk over to the counter once more and deposit a second batch of small toys for me to price. I happily do so as it gives me something to do with my hands and an excuse to change the topic of the conversation.

"You're buying a lot of toys today. Is it a special occasion?"

"No, just Thursday..."

The older woman who is also browsing for toys for her grandson approaches the counter and presents me with a teddy bear.

"Hello again, Miss Betty! That's such a great choice. Jeremy is going to love it!"

There is an awkward moment of silence between the three of us until Miss Betty speaks up with a fresh piece of gossip.

"Have you heard about the new man in town, ladies?"

Once again, I try not to roll my eyes, but Mrs. Paulson immediately straightens her back and widens her eyes, careful to catch every crumb of information coming her way.

"What? Who's that? Who is he, Miss Betty?" she asks.

"Probably the new fellow they sent to collect the garbage and keep the beach clean," I reply and try not to giggle.

"Oh, nothing like that, Tiffany. He's a proper gentleman," Miss Betty replies. "Yes, yes. He's the new Literature teacher up at the school. He came here on some sort of program they have there and, wouldn't you know it, he used to be a professor at North Newport College."

"North Newport? What do you mean, used to be?" I ask, getting more and more involved in this local piece of gossip even though I don't want to.

"Well, I think that he's going for... what do you call it? A doctoral diploma or something like that? The girls at the bakery explained it all to me this morning, but I didn't get it, to be honest. All in all, this is important for his career. His position here at the Yellow Point school will count for his doctorate program somehow. I'm not sure you can be a doctor of just Literature though, can you?"

"Yes of course, it's a PhD so he'd be able to be called doctor, but it's definitely different than a medical doctor. I went to North Newport too. " I offer but neither of the two women is interested.

"How come the girls at the bakery know so much about him?" Mrs. Paulson asks.

"Ah, he was in there just this morning, buying himself a bit of breakfast. He just arrived in town and is trying to move all his things. But those girls were in such a state! According to them, he's a real looker!" Miss Betty giggles, and, despite her age, she still blushes at the thought of a handsome man who just came to live in Yellow Point.

"Well, I think I'm going to have to keep my eyes open for him, aren't I?" Mrs. Paulson says and grins.

"You're married though, right Mrs. Paulson?" I ask.

"Umm... Yes of course, not to meet for that reason exactly. I meant... I need to meet him because my children... Yes, my boys will attend the Yellow Point school. I'm sure he would like to meet me and have a chat about the... what do you call it? The thing... the..."

"Curriculum?" I venture a guess, even though I can see that she's making it up as she goes along, inventing wildly.

"That's it! I need to talk to this new teacher about the curriculime," she replies and mispronounces the word.

"Yes. And when you see him, make sure to lead with that," I advise, feeling a little cheeky. She doesn't catch it and I hand her the bags full of toys, eager for this interaction to be over.

"How about you, Tiffany? Aren't you interested in this new man in town? Especially now that you're single?" Miss Betty asks me.

I sigh to myself, thinking just how awful it is to be pushed from one man to the other. This traditional concept that you cannot be single even for a moment. The very instant a man shows up on the horizon, you have to jump on him like he's a gazelle at a water clearing.

"What? I don't know a single thing about this mystery man. Miss Betty, like I said, I don't want to rush things. I'm fine on my own."

"So... you want to be alone?"

"Not forever," I smile. "I just want to make sure that the next man I date is the right one. I just don't want to set myself for more disappointment, that's all. And I am aware that might take some time or some searching but if that's the way it has to be, I'm fine with that."

"I guess you know best, dear," she adds and turns to leave the store.

Mrs. Paulson has already disappeared with her boys. As soon as she heard the piece of gossip about the new Literature teacher, she found something much better to do with her day. Miss Betty lingers for a moment longer in the door of the toy store and watches me with her aged, milky but wise eyes.

"Is there something wrong, Miss Betty?"

"No. Just thinking about what you said, dear. You know, life has a funny way, Tiffany. Even if you don't believe it because you're so young, life has a funny way of throwing things in our path. Sometimes, it's best to just... let them happen."

She gives me a small smile and walks away, leaving me alone to my thoughts and my desire of getting back to my book, The Sun Also Rises by Hemingway. Nothing like spending time vicariously in the 1920's to dull the persistent ache of current days.

CHAPTER TWO

Possibilites

TYLER

I don't know if it's the fact that I'm new to Yellow Point or if it's the massive truck parked in front of the house containing all my stuff, but everyone has been staring at me like I'm an alien the entire day.

"Hello! How may I help you... Sir? Mister? Mmm... Or... what should I call you? Do you have a name?" she giggles and blushes, fidgeting behind the counter while the other girl wiping tables is now completely motionless, watching our interaction.

I feel like I've stumbled on an episode of *The Twilight Zone*.

"You can call me whatever you want," I try to smile even though I still don't understand what's happening. "My name is Tyler, by the way."

The girl behind the counter of the coffee shop starts to laugh incredibly loudly and dramatically even though there was nothing funny about what I just said.

"Oh... Oh, my God... Stop it! Stop it, Tyler! You're so funny! Wow!"

"Thank you? Anyway... I would like a..."

"My name is Andrea, by the way," the girl behind the counter says and tucks a strand of hair behind her ear in a gesture which is supposed to be seductive. I understand that she's flirting with me.

"Hello, Andrea. As I was saying, can I have a cappuccino with a little cinnamon on top?"

"Oh, my God! That's my favorite drink as well!!" she exclaims.

I don't believe her.

"Well... how about that? A coincidence," I reply as cordially as I can.

She turns around and starts to make my drink but cannot peel her eyes off me to the extent that I feel somewhat uncomfortable.

"Here you go... Tyler," she adds in a softer tone of voice, still flirting with me.

"Thanks!" I reply, not wanting to encourage it.

I leave the coffee shop and head back toward my new house, where I still have so many things to unpack. What is happening in this town? First the girls at the bakery this morning who couldn't stop giggling while I was getting a couple of bagels, then that woman who was carrying a gigantic bag of toys and who almost followed me home, and now this girl at the coffee shop. Are they truly not used to strangers here, in Yellow Point?

While these musings roll around in my head, I sip my cappuccino and make my way to the new house.

I turn a corner and enjoy the salty smell coming from the sea. Behind this row of houses, a small and bohemian beach lies dormant in the late August sun, still baking in the heat. All I can think about is taking a swim. After all, the weather will turn soon when August is over, and I won't be able to enjoy the water anymore. Unpacking can wait, I decide. I need a beach break.

Inside the house, I rummage through a few of the boxes that I managed to unload from the truck and locate a pair of swimming trunks. They're not my favorite, but they will have to do for now. The afternoon sun is dying and with it, the sweet August heat. I go out through the back door and head down the overgrown pathway toward the beach.

The smell of hot sand and brine brings a special happiness to my soul that is difficult to put into words. As a literature professor, I know that so many authors over the centuries have been in love with the sea and its mesmerizing beauty. Endless quotes from James Joyce, Jules Verne, Kate Chopin, even Jacques Cousteau roll through my head now and I feel happier than I've been in years. Then I remember a John F. Kennedy quote, *"And it is an interesting biological fact that all of us have, in our veins the exact same percentage of salt in our blood that exists in the ocean, and, therefore, we have salt in our blood, in our sweat, in our tears. We are tied to the ocean. And when we go back to the sea, whether it is to sail or to watch it, we are going back from whence we came."*

Yes, I'm going back from whence I came, for the whole afternoon if I can get away with it. Living in the big city may make your dreams come true but, perhaps, true happiness does indeed lie in the small things. I had a student once who talked very highly of this town, and I have always been curious.

The beach is not big or very touristy. Just enough to satisfy your craving of sun, sand, and waves. I take off my shoes, throw the towel into the sand and take a plunge. The water is surprisingly cold but refreshing in the September heat.

After swimming around, investigating seashells, and letting the waves carry me around for the better part of an hour, I sit pensive on the shoreline, resting and watching the waves swell a ways out to the horizon, then gather speed and roll up on to the shore, lapping at my body. My thoughts are tamed by the water and I let my mind empty, enjoying just *being*.

Suddenly a group of what looks like teenage girls has formed on the beach, close to where I sit with my towel and shoes behind me. I can hear them giggling and talking fast. Finally, one of them addresses me.

"Hi. We have a question. My friend here works at the bakery, and she thinks she saw you there and that you are going to be the new teacher at our school. Is that true?"

"Yes, I am. Honestly, I wish we could have met in a different circumstance, but here we are. I'm Tyler Stone, girls, new Literature teacher at the high school," I reply, not feeling entirely happy that my solitude has been interrupted.

"Did you just move here?"

"Yes. I used to teach at North Newport College," I reply, still feeling slightly awkward. I pat myself dry with the towel and the girls keep staring at me and giggling.

"Wow! That's a big school! Did you also like... go there?" they struggle to keep the conversation going while I put my T-shirt back on and get ready to leave.

"Do you mean if I also attended North Newport? No, I went to Oxford. Girls, thank you for your interest and I hope we can talk more once the school year starts shortly. I have some more unpacking to do so... if you'll excuse me..."

They throw some more comments my way which get lost in the wind and the tide. I walk back up the path, a bit peeved at the fact that they interrupted my afternoon tranquility. Still, the part about the unpacking was true.

Before I have a chance to walk back into the house, the driver of the truck, a man in his sixties with a comical comb over and a Led Zeppelin T-shirt meets me halfway.

"How's it going, Teach'? Been to the beach yet?"

"Good afternoon, Sam! Yes, I've just been down there for a swim. Yes, it's incredible. I feel so lucky that I have a beach all to myself now. It's almost unreal!" I reply.

"I suppose you don't get something like this in the big city, do ya?" he grins.

"I guess we don't. All we have are pools and health clubs. You have to pay an arm and a leg to go there twice a week. And now... look at this!" I point toward the sea behind me.

"Is this why you moved here?" he asks me as he starts to move some more of the boxes out of the truck.

"Not exactly. It was mostly my job. I teach at North Newport College, and this was an amazing opportunity for me," I explain.

He stops and wipes sweat off his forehead in a universal gesture that all workmen do.

"This?! Yellow Point was an amazing opportunity for you?"

"Yes, Sam," I laugh seeing the confusion on the man's face. "The college has a wonderful program through which the students at the Yellow Point school can take advanced classes. College level classes, I mean. It gives them a bit of a head start on college credits. As for me, if the program is successful, I'm in line for a promotion."

"Ah, I see what you mean Teach'..." he groans and hands me one of the boxes labelled *books*. "What is in here – rocks?"

"Just books, Sam..."

"So, anyway, do you like Yellow Point, then?" he asks me.

"I've only been here for a few hours. Since this morning. The town in itself is fantastic. What could compete with the small streets, the quaint houses, the view of the sea? But..."

The man stops and stares at me.

"What is it?"

"Some of the people have been giving me strange looks. The girls at the bakery, a woman and her children, this group of teenage girls that was practically stalking me at the beach. I don't know what to make of it all."

He tries to process what I've just told him.

"Huh. So... all of these people were... women, then?" he grins.

"Yes. Why?"

"Well, Teach' it seems to me like you've got yourself a few fans here in Yellow Point."

"What are you talking about?" I ask.

"Come on. You come from the big city. You're an experienced man. What are you, late forties, fifty maybe? This is not your first rodeo if you know what I mean. You have a mirror, right?" he laughs.

"Sam, what are you getting at?"

"Teach' you moving here, to Yellow Point is like.. . George Clooney moving here. Or, what's his name? The fellow who plays James Bond. My wife goes into a frenzy every time he's on!"

"Well I don't know if *that's* the case. Most likely, I'm new to Yellow Point and I come from the city. People must be curious. Not to mention that I will be working at the school, and they must want to get to know me on account of their children."

The man finishes unloading the last of the boxes and deposits it in my hallway.

"Oh don't be so naïve. It doesn't look good on a man your age," he chuckles. "Plus, look on the bright side. Maybe this will be good for you."

"What do you mean?"

He gets into the truck and slams the old door.

"Teach'... I guess some things you can't learn from books."

I am left thinking about the man's words. As I close the door behind me, the house seems a little less empty now that all my things are in. They are still in boxes but at least my life is all here now.

My life in boxes.

Before I can start unpacking and finding a proper place for everything, I decide to take a shower. The saltwater needs to be rinsed off and I feel a desperate need to clean up before I can do more physical work. In the small bathroom, I turn the shower knob but can only hear a faint rustle.

"No... no... please, don't do this to me. Not the shower! Anything but the shower!" I pray in desperation.

I start turning the knobs every which way but nothing works. What am I supposed to do now? I've only been in Yellow Point for a few hours and have no clue if I can find a plumber so late in the afternoon. Deeply frustrated, I go back downstairs and find my phone. The only contact I have in Yellow Point is Sam, who has just left with his truck and, of course, the principal of the Yellow Point school.

I realize that I can't call the principal to tell him that my shower is broken. This cannot be an interaction we have even before the school year starts so, Sam it is, then.

"Hello, Sam? Yeah, it's me, Tyler Stone."

"Hello, Teach! Did I forget something?"

"No, no. But... my shower isn't working, and I thought that, perhaps, you know a plumber here in Yellow Point who can help me."

I try to explain my predicament as quickly as possible.

"I do know a plumber. That would be Gary up on Fisher Street."

"Wonderful! Can you give me his number, please?"

"Sure! But he's away. He's taken his family to Dolly-wood theme park over in Tennessee," Sam says.

"No... is there anyone else?"

"Not that I know of. Look, many of these houses are old, and you need someone good to take a real look at that plumbing. I suggest you wait for Gary to come back from Dollywood, and he'll sort it out for you nice and good."

"And until then? How will I shower, Sam?"

"Just go next door," the man says as if it's the easiest solution in the world and I'm silly for not having thought about it.

"Next door? But I don't know anyone!" I protest.

"No need! Everyone is friendly here. Oh, but don't go to your right. That's Mrs. Galen. She's... well... she only likes her cats and chances are you will come out of her house smelling worse than you went in. Go to your other neighbor, ok? I have to go now. Good luck with the shower!"

"No, wait! Who is the other neighbor? Do I need to know something about..."

Too late. Sam has already hung up, leaving me to wonder about what I should do.

Apparently, to my right there is a woman who won't welcome me and to my left, there is a mysterious neighbor that I have to try my luck with. I scratch my head figuring out if I should bring them something. But then again, I have nothing to bring even if I wanted. All my things are in boxes.

Bracing myself, I grab my towel and head next door. After all, what could happen? The worst is that they could say no. That's not so bad.

I knock on the door and can feel my heart rate going up. Only a moment later, the door opens, and I have the shock of a lifetime. I struggle to understand what's happening and feel as if my heart has now completely stopped. What the...but... how is this *possible*? Time literally stops and then ten years disappears in an instant, and I find myself speechless, staring into the same set of eyes that pulled me in to that strange vortex so many years ago, swirling and moving in and in and in through her eyes, trapping my soul in the most ecstatic of places. Glue. It feels like glue, and I must force myself to find my own place, to ground myself in the reality that brought me to this person's door. Shaking my head, I back up and look around for a brief moment, checking that reality is still reality.

"Tiffany?!"

CHAPTER THREE

Showers

TIFFANY

"Are you done for the day, then Tiffany?" Abbey asks me as we both walk down the street toward the town center. She looks somewhat tired but still cheerful and in a good mood.

"Yes. I decided to close the toy store for the day," I reply yawning.

"Didn't you say you were doing inventory tonight?"

"That was the plan. But... I don't know. It suddenly felt so lonely and closed off in there. I think I just want to go home, order a pizza, and take a hot bath. The inventory audit can wait," I reply.

"Is this about... Brian?" Abbey asks me with a dose of cautiousness in her voice.

As a close friend, she knows that this is a touchy subject for me.

"In a way. I don't miss him or anything like that if that was what you were wondering. Mrs. Paulson came in the toy store today with her boys..."

"Ugghh..." Abbey replies and makes a face as if she has just stepped in something bad.

"I know but what can I do? She's one of my best customers. Anyway. So, she comes in today and starts grilling me about Brian, right?"

"What business is it of hers how things are between you and Brian?" I just don't get that woman," Abbey says and groans.

"You're right but that's not the point. Her questions or her prying didn't bother me that much. What upset me most was the fact that she refused to believe that I was the one who left Brian. Even though she is well aware that he cheated on me."

"What do you mean? She thinks he broke up with you?" Abbey asks.

"I have no clue. I told her that I want to take my time and not rush into another relationship. She looked like I just told her I want to go to the moon wearing an outfit made of tin foil."

Abbey laughs as we reach the corner of the street where we are supposed to part ways for the day.

"Well, it makes sense. I don't think a woman like her can envision life without a man," Abbey says.

"Yeah. Even if it is someone like Brian. Anyway, I'm going home."

"Me too. Enjoy your bath and pizza!"

She gives me a short hug and walks briskly down a smaller street that I know will take her to her house. Ever since we were little girls, Abbey and I have been walking the same streets in Yellow Point it seems. Nothing has changed and, perhaps, nothing ever will. I don't know if it's a good thing or a bad thing. Perhaps a bit of both.

I walk down my own alley covered in small pebbles. They are white and rounded now, the wind across the sea and the endless brine having worked their magic on the very stones of Yellow Point. I notice with some degree of curiosity that the lights are on in the house next door to mine. It has been silent and empty for a while now, so this is an interesting development. Or, at least, what passes for interesting in a small sea town like Yellow Point.

But I only care about my pizza and bath. Once inside, I turn on my own lights and place an order for a large cheese pizza that is bound to satisfy my craving for salt and dairy. Without wasting any time, I head upstairs and plan to eat the pizza in the bathtub, for the ultimate relaxation experience. Before I can reach the landing, the doorbell rings and I'm surprised at just how fast they managed to deliver my pie.

"Wow, I knew you guys were fast, but this must be some kind of record!" I exclaim as I open the door.

My heart beats out of control for a moment and then stops completely. For the first time in my entire life, I can hear the blood rushing through my veins and under my skin, numbing me and making my head go dizzy. I try to make sense of what I'm seeing on my doorstep but it's almost impossible.

I feel paralyzed and my mouth has gone completely dry like after drinking something bitter and strange. Even though I try to swallow, it has no effect on me and my throat seems constricted, no air coming through.

"What... is... is this... a joke? How is this... possible? What are you doing here? How come you're here?" I babble as I stare at the man on my doorstep.

He's wearing an old T-shirt, vintage jeans, and a pair of black flip flops. His salt and pepper hair is slicked back and his dark eyes are, I presume, just as wide as mine.

"Tiffany?!"

"Professor Stone?"

"This is... weird..." I manage to say a few more words as we stare at each other, not knowing what to make of this.

"I agree, in fact. When I came over to knock on my neighbor's door, I did not, in a million years, expect that Tiffany Hart would be the one to open. What are the chances? Tiffany Hart..." he says, not peeling his eyes off me.

"But I just don't understand. What are you doing here, Professor Stone?"

"Umm... this is going to sound... well, crazy, because it is. Maybe it isn't, and it's just life throwing you one of those odd curveballs. But I moved next door to you, Tiffany. And, as it turns out, the house is fantastically old and hasn't been looked after in a while. The shower is not working at all. And I had a swim earlier and worked on moving all my boxes inside. So now I need to take a shower," he explains.

My mind keeps racing, and my thoughts go in and out of focus as he talks. All I can think about is how good he looks. Even though I haven't seen him in almost ten years, Professor Stone has not changed at all. In fact, the small things that might have altered here and there only serve to make him even more handsome than he was back in my years in college.

"...so that's why I came," he finishes explaining as I focus back on his words.

"Oh, I see. Yeah, that makes sense, I guess. It's just so crazy!"

"I agree. Can I come in?" he asks.

"Oh, my God! Yes, of course. I apologize, Professor Stone. Come in, sure. You can take a shower as well if you want," I reply and welcome him into the living room.

He smiles warmly and his dark eyes fixate on my eyes in the same way they used to do when I was nineteen and in college. I get a rush of excitement and my insides squirm. Professor Stone still has the same power over me that he had ten years ago.

"Tiffany," he addresses me in a velvety voice.

"Yes?"

"I would love it if you stopped calling me Professor Stone," he smiles. "I'm happy that you have the same level of respect for me you once had but... things are different now, aren't they?" he adds in a throaty whisper.

"Ummm... what? Different? Different how?"

"Well, you're no longer in college and I am not your *professor* anymore. Here we are, in your living room, of all places."

"Oh, yes! Yes... That's what you mean. I thought... Never mind what I thought. Yes!"

I try to gloss over the fact that my mind was already filling up with fantasies about the handsome man standing in front of me right now.

"Well, now that we've found each other again, shall we reconnect a little, Tiffany?" he asks and smiles. I am very unsure whether or not he's flirting. Much like I was in college.

"I guess we should, Profess... Tyler," I correct myself. "That feels strange. Calling you Tyler."

"Don't worry. You'll get used to it," he adds in his deadly low voice that sends shivers down my spine.

This used to be my daily game in my college years, I recall as I walk into the kitchen to retrieve a bottle of wine and two glasses. Ever since we met, Professor Stone or, Tyler as I am now supposed to call him, has been playing a fox and hunter game with me that has been both enticing and confusing at the same time. Isn't desire always like that? No idea if he meant to, I'm sure only of how it felt.

And now, here he is, in my living room, his behavior not having changed a bit.

"Do you like red wine? I can't recall," I say as I hand him one of the glasses.

"It's perfect. Thank you, Tiffany."

He makes room for me on the couch and welcomes me next to him. Even though this is my house and my living room, it's more than obvious that he has taken the reins of our accidental meeting. His confidence and manly charm leave no room for interpretation or second guessing.

"Tell me, then Tyler. What have you been doing in these past ten years? And what are you doing here, in Yellow Point? I suppose you're the new Literature teacher that everyone is talking about?" I ask and know that I am flirting with him as well and not of my own volition. This is just how my body reacts to him.

"Ah, so I'm famous here already!" he laughs as he shakes his head. "I hope that I can live up to that fame, Tiffany."

"I don't see why not. All you have to do is... be yourself, Tyler," I flirt more. He smiles and sips his red wine.

"Thank you. That's such a wonderful compliment. Yellow Point is a small town, however. As you know."

"Is that not the reason why you came here?" I ask, eager to find out as much as possible now.

"Partly. I'm here because I believe that small schools deserve more. And the students who attend schools such as the one in Yellow Point need more visibility. I'm afraid that they often get overlooked when it comes time to apply for a good college, scholarships, or grants. So, the program that North Newport has in place aims to provide them with advanced classes that will educate them at a superior level and, of course, look very good on their college applications. And I seem to remember a clever girl some years ago in one of my classes that really talked the place up."

"Yes, it is! And that is an incredible thing to do, Tyler," I listen to him enraptured, absorbing every word out of his mouth just like I did when I was a teenager. "And what's in it for you?"

"The pleasure of teaching the students of Yellow Point. A new challenge, the experience of teaching in a small town... And a promotion if the program goes well," he says.

"Then I sincerely hope you get it!" I reply and touch my wine glass to his as a sign of good fortune.

"You're so kind, Tiffany!"

"Still, you haven't told me what you've been up to in the past ten years, though," I keep circling around the same topic, hoping that my interest is not so obvious. Naturally, I want to know if he has gotten married in the meantime or not. If there's a wife waiting for him back in the city or, worse, next door while he's here having red wine with me.

"Tiffany, your interest flatters me. A woman such as yourself showing so much grace and taking interest in a man who just emerged from the dark recesses our the past unexpectedly. How could I repay you?"

"You're just as smooth talking as ever, Tyler. Do you know that?"

He grins and drinks a little more wine.

"Mmm... The past ten years have been uneventful for me, Tiffany. I've been teaching at North Newport as you know and I'm working on a book about the life of Jane Austen, her personal life specifically because all the books recount just the basics about her. I'm hoping to have it published in the next two years. Other than that, I've traveled a fair bit. To England, of course, to research my book. But for pleasure as well. I've been to India..."

"Oh, A Passage to India, then?" I reply and try to impress him with my literary knowledge just like I used to do ten years ago.

His entire face lights up at my mention.

"Well done, Tiffany! That's incredible! You still remember my lectures, I see?"

In reality, I remember the way he looked on the day he gave a lecture about this book ten years ago. There was something about his dark eyes, the passion with which he spoke, the movement of his hands through the air that had my mind and my soul mesmerized.

"Of course. I remember all your lectures. Professor..." I add on a cheeky voice.

"Then I might have to quiz you later," he flirts back and moves a little closer to me on the couch.

"Why? Do you think I'm lying? Why would I do that? Oh, to impress you, right?" I grin.

"Perhaps you're right, Tiffany. Or maybe you have something else on your mind entirely," he says.

"Oh, yeah? What would that be... Professor?"

We look at each other for a few moments, aware that the temperature in the room has just gone up a few degrees. It could be the wine but the electricity between us is buzzing more than ever.

The doorbell rings again and pulls us out of this enchantment. He looks around, wondering what to do but I reassure him.

"It's just the pizza I ordered earlier. I'll go and get it!"

As I take care of the pizza, I realize that he doesn't know anything about me either. Did he imagine that the doorbell late in the evening is a boyfriend I could have? A husband of mine that is coming home after a day's work and has forgotten his key?

"I ordered a pizza earlier and I guess it took them a while to arrive. Anyway..."

"So, what about you, Tiffany? What have you been doing since college?" he asks right on cue, confirming my thoughts.

"Well, after graduation, I wanted to continue and study journalism. I saw myself as the next big thing, writing incisive articles and getting published in The New York Times. I dreamed about winning the Pulitzer Prize and stumbling over a big scoop. Like the Sackler family and the opioid crisis or Sam Giancana and the CIA or... you get the point."

He smiles and nods, licking his fingers as he eats a slice of the cheese loaded pizza.

"Are these scoops or conspiracy theories, Tiffany?"

"Are we friends now or are you still my professor, Tyler?" I bite back and he starts laughing and my quickness.

"Alright, alright. You win!" he says.

"And no, they are not conspiracy theories. Both of them are real. Anyway, that's not the point. I dreamed about doing something like that."

"What happened? Why didn't you?"

"My health. My asthma seemed to get worse and worse over the years. I returned to Yellow Point to focus on my health. The doctors told me that the weather here is milder and won't affect me as much. They also said that I shouldn't overextend myself and just take it easy. It was a blow, but I learned to live with it."

"How are you feeling now?" he asks, and I am happy to see genuine concern etched on his handsome face.

"Things are under control. A few years back, a good friend of mine, June, came back to Yellow Point. After her aunt died she inherited her house, her toy store, and some money. June got married to her high school sweetheart, Trent, and they moved to Paris. But she left me in charge of the toy store and was kind enough to help me pay for treatment, which really helped tremendously. As a result, here I am, fit as a fiddle and the manager of a toy store that I adore!"

"*I may not have gone where I intended to go, but I think I have ended up where I needed to be*," Tyler says, giving me a splendid quote that sums up my life journey so far.

"Douglas Adams! *The Long Dark Tea-Time of the Soul!* I love that book! I love that entire series. It's so funny!" I exclaim, feeling bubbly and warm inside like a bottle of rich champagne has just been opened inside my heart.

He puts down his plate, stands up, and starts to clap, taking me by surprise.

"Tiffany, you are – unbelievable! Without a doubt, the best student that I have ever had! And the fact that you still remember all that makes me... I feel like I could just..."

He stops and looks at me, unsure how to continue.

"Have another glass of wine?" I offer and smile.

"That sounds excellent," he says, relieved. "And perhaps get that shower I was talking about."

Chapter Four

Standup

Tyler

The school in Yellow Point is just as I expected it to be. I've never seen it before as I only ever interviewed with the principal over the internet in calls, but nothing about its appearance surprises me. A low and squat building with a single floor that serves to teach the few, perhaps tens of students of this small but charming seaside town.

The courtyard and adjacent streets are empty as I walk toward it, early in the morning, the late August sun already burning my face and the cup of to go coffee scolding my fingers. The school year hasn't started yet but we, the teachers, are meeting beforehand to discuss the curriculum and receive any type of news or directions that the principal has for us and the following year.

A light blue car stops a few feet from me and a man who seems to be in his forties emerges. He waves at me and smiles broadly. The innate happiness and familiarity of small-town people never cease to amaze me.

"Hello, there! Are you the new Literature teacher?" he asks me as he continues to wave even though I've already spotted him.

"Good morning! Yes, I'm Tyler Stone. How are you?"

"Fine, fine, can't complain. I'm John Dodgson, the chemistry teacher myself," the man beams at me and shakes my hand very vigorously.

We walk together through the fenced courtyard and enter the refreshing and cool halls of the school.

"To be honest, I'm happy I bumped into you, John. I was wondering if any of the teachers would be willing to show me around."

"No worries, Tyler. We're all very friendly here, in Yellow Point! Yes, of course I'll show you around. And any questions you have, send them my way!" John replies.

He leads me toward the main staff room which is still empty.

"Look at that! It looks like we're the first ones here, Tyler!" he exclaims and pats my back in a very fatherly way even though he's younger than me.

"I suppose it's still early. It's not even nine in the morning yet," I reply.

"Yes... the others are still in vacation mode. Or as the youngsters might say – vaycay," he laughs at his own joke and his big, brushy mustache trembles.

This guy, friendly enough for sure, is a bit 'extra' and I'm certain that *that* is what the so-called youngsters would say. The term 'vaycay' is in wider use that he must realize.

"How about a cup of Joe, Tyler?" John asks me.

"Sure. Thanks!" I reply, even though it's more than obvious that I already have a to-go cup of coffee in my hand.

But I don't want to say no or be impolite, so I accept. John hurries over to the coffee machine and starts pressing a bunch of buttons.

"I never know how to work this thing. This... newfangled technology they have nowadays is going to kill us!"

"Yeah coffee machines can be deadly. Tell you what, John. If it rises and comes at us with a vengeance, I'll unplug it for you," I joke.

We spend the next few moments in silence as he manages to get the coffee going. I take a seat at one of the three round tables in the teachers' room and think how long it's been since that coffee machine was cleaned. After all, it's been sitting there over the summer with no one touching it.

"Tell me, John, have you been a chemistry teacher here long?"

"Oh, yes! I suppose it's closing in on twenty years now."

"Really? That long?"

"Absolutely. After I got my degree, I came right back to Yellow Point and applied for the job. The principal back then was Miss Florence. A bit of a pain she was, if you ask me. But she was happy to give me the position. I always wanted to be a teacher here," he smiles.

"I'm glad that you saw your dream come true, John," I reply and mean it.

"Ah thank you, Tyler. What about you, then? Are you here on the program?" he asks me, clearly knowing more than anyone else in town.

"Yes, yes, I am. North Newport College gave me this opportunity and I thought it was a great idea."

"And how are you getting along in town, then?" he asks and sits across from me in one of the classic, plastic school chairs that are supposed to take everything a student can throw at them.

"I've only been here for two days. So far, all I've managed to do is to unpack my things to some extent and realize that my shower doesn't work. But the plumber is off on vacation with his family to Dollyhood or Hollywood or some other theme park or somewhere. Now I have to wait until he comes back."

"Dollywood probably. It's just over in Tennessee; Dolly Parton's place. Yeah that's a pickle, then," John replies. "What have you been doing? If you don't mind my asking."

"Not at all. I went to Tiffany's house, my next door neighbor. She let me use her shower and told me that I can come back whenever needed. I suppose that will have to do for now," I explain.

John, the chemistry teacher gives me an odd look when I mention Tiffany, which I can't quite comprehend.

"Ah... your neighbor. Yes. This is the Hart girl, isn't it? She has the toy store downtown, yeah?"

"Yes, I suppose that's her. Why?"

"No reason, Tyler, no reason."

He sips his coffee but continues to peer at me over the top of his mug.

"Do you know what's funny about this whole situation? I knocked on her door thinking that she is just my neighbor but, as it turns out, we already knew each other," I start.

"How do you mean?"

"Tiffany and I go way back. She was in my Literature class in college. Tiffany attended North Newport and she was one of the best, I might add. It was so strange, uncanny I could say, to see that door open and then... there was her face. Tiffany. Like a ghost emerging from the sands of time," I muse as Tiffany's face appears in my mind's eye.

John stares at me, unsure of what to make of all this.

"So, you're telling me that you two have known each other for ten years?" he asks.

"Sort of – in a manner of speaking. We lost contact after she graduated but, yes. Tiffany and I have a connection from the past, I guess. Isn't she a lovely girl? I spent the evening with her when I went to ask if I could use her shower and it was the best night, I've had in... years, maybe. I suppose I forgot how easy it can be talking to a woman. To an old friend."

John puts down the coffee cup and leans in closer to me.

"Are you married, Tyler?" he asks me. "Is there a Mrs. Stone somewhere in the big city?"

"No. I've never been married."

"Ah, by choice then?"

"Well, I suppose I never found the right person," I try to keep the conversation casual and light, even though John's questions have become too personal for my taste. "And I don't believe in the idea that you should marry someone just because you have to. Because society says so. I guess I've been waiting to find... my person."

He stirs awkwardly on the childish plastic chair and looks toward the door of the teachers' room as if he's wondering who could be listening on the other side.

"I see. And are you planning on getting married? Back in the city?" he asks me.

"Like I said, I haven't met anyone who has made me want to get married. And right now, I'm not even dating. How could I get married, John?" I laugh.

We sit in silence for a few more seconds. I haven't touched the cup of coffee that John handed me, and I was right. There is a layer of dust at the top floating around.

"How long has Tiffany had the toy store? It's doing well here in Yellow Point?" I ask him.

"She's had it for about two years now. The store is successful I would say, yes. As it turns out, she has a flair for business that one, and she's managed to turn that old place into a real point of attraction. People from two towns over come to buy Christmas presents here, birthday presents, and whatnot. In fact, it's such an attraction that the mayor is now taking advantage of the traffic to her toy store and other downtown businesses and they're organizing a Christmas market. To support the town economy, have people buy tickets to rides and... you get the point; it will be a whole new festival for Yellow Point."

"I had no idea! That's great. She didn't mention much about the toy store. But I'm happy to find out that her ideas are not only driving her business but also benefiting the town."

"Yes, yes. She's a real brainiac, that one," John replies and pours himself another cup of coffee as we wait for the other teachers and the principal to arrive.

"How about her... umm... you know...has she ever been married? Is she seeing someone?" I ask him.

"She has never been married and she isn't seeing anyone right now that we know of here in Yellow Point," John replies and for the first time ever, I am happy for the small-town grapevine that carries this news and bits of gossip.

"So, she's single, then?"

"Well, there was Brian."

My heart jumps and I can feel my senses waking up to this interesting development.

"Brian? Who is this Brian?" I hear myself asking.

"He's the Fowler's boy. Their son. His mother, Gina Fowler is a nurse here in Yellow Point and has been for thirty years. And his father, Tony, is..."

"But what happened between Brian and Tiffany?" I interrupt John, not being too interested in Brian's family tree.

"I suppose... They had a relationship for a long time. Years, it seems to me, although I wouldn't be able to tell you exactly how many. And then, well..."

"What? What happened?" I feel myself getting more and more involved in the story.

"Brian seems to have had a bit of a business with a waitress at that new restaurant over in Frazier, Mad something. Mad Cactus! I don't know if that's true or not. Of course, Tiffany said that she caught Brian and this waitress red-handed, doing things... well, you can imagine," he says and clears his throat, the conversation now making him uncomfortable. "But I don't know if that is to be believed."

"What do you mean, John? Why would she lie?"

"Eh... you know how women are. Nothing is ever good enough for them."

I sit there, staring John in the face, shocked at his blatant sexism. Still, I need to know more.

"I don't know that I'd agree with that, John. So that ended things, I take it."

"Something like that. Tiffany had Brian packing. Sent him back to his parent's place I think. They were supposed to get married, but she broke it all off. I don't know why she did that. A good man like Brian..."

"A good man like Brian?" I repeat his words not believing what I'm hearing. "Tiffany caught him cheating on her with a random waitress. Would a good man do that?"

"I don't know Tyler. But what I do know is that a good woman closes her eyes. Yes," he replies stupidly.

"To this? So that he can turn around and do it again? With all the other waitresses between here and Frazier?" My eyebrows are now making a new home on the top of my head. I can't hide the shock of his statement and I don't know that my eyebrows will settle back to normal and stop questioning what I'm hearing.

"Well, now she's alone and almost thirty. What good is that?" John says and sips his dirty coffee.

There are several things I would like to reply to his comment but all of them would likely result in a permanent sense of animosity between me and the only teacher I've had a conversation with so far. I don't want to start off on the wrong foot before the school year has even commenced.

"John, can you tell me why Tiffany..."

But he sets the coffee cup on the table with a firm hand and points toward the window with his thumb. I look out and see two cars pulling into the school's parking lot.

"Who is that?" I ask, wondering why he'd need to point at teachers arriving as expected.

"Some of the other teachers. Tyler, look... This interest you have in Tiffany. Maybe it's not the best idea," he says in a hushed tone even though it's still just the two of us in the teachers' room.

"What do you mean?"

"Tyler, this is not the big city anymore. This is Yellow Point. And Tiffany is what, fifteen years younger than you? People here are not going to like... whatever it is that you have going on."

"There is nothing going on!" I laugh, not being able to believe what I'm hearing.

"Is that right? Because Tommy said that you spent hours at her house the other night and that you were very cozy on the couch with wine and everything."

"Tommy? Who is Tommy?" I ask, barely hiding my annoyance.

"That sixteen-year-old kid who delivers pizza and who always smells like cinnamon, for some reason," John replies, completely oblivious to what the teenager is doing.

"That's not... cinnamon, John."

"What do you mean?"

"It doesn't matter, that's not the point. I don't know what Johnny from the pizza place told you or... the entire town it seems, but nothing happened between me and Tiffany. Yes, we spent some time together and yes, we had wine. But, like I said, we are two old friends catching up. She was my student in college. She was in my class. No big deal."

"Tyler, I understand what you're saying. But that's now how people will see it. Your interest in a girl that's so much younger than you and, even more worrisome, one who used to be your student back in the day will make Yellow Point see you in a different light," he tries to explain.

"A different light?"

"You're a teacher here now, Tyler. People are meant to trust you. To trust that you will educate their children and that you're a standup guy."

"And I might not be a standup guy if I were caught catching up with an old friend over wine?" I ask feeling irked by his comment. Damn. Maybe this whole Yellow

Point thing is a giant mistake if this is how this town thinks.

"Not if you're interested in girls that are fifteen and twenty years younger than you. Not to mention the project that was set up by the college. It could damage your career. If the school here gives you a bad review at the end of the year on account of your... dealings with a former student, then it could really damage your path to success, Professor. I mean, why risk it, right? Is that what you want?"

Before I have a chance to respond to his limited, severely asinine comments and make a likely ineffective attempt to correct his thinking, two women walk into the teachers' lounge. They are both holding cups of coffee and break into wide grins the moment they notice me.

"Well hello hello! You must be Tyler Stone! Our new teacher!" one of them beams.

"Yes, the one and only," I smile and try to match their enthusiasm and wonder if I'm succeeding.

"Yeah I bet once the school year starts, all the girls are going to fight to be in your class!"

Chapter Five

Disclosures

Tiffany

The library is cool and silent, as usual. After the noise and bustle of the street, I gather my thoughts and walk toward the little office at the back where Abbey usually spends her w o r k - day.

"Hey, can I come in?" I ask her.

She looks up from an old registry and smiles, removing the sole ear bud from her ear as the other one dangles, swinging back and forth as she moves.

"Yes, of course! Hi! I wasn't expecting you this morning was I?"

"Nah. I just thought you might need a break," I reply and hand her a to-go cup of coffee. "Here, I got your favorite. It has a shot of hot chocolate and some peppermint."

Abbey inhales the aroma and takes a sip.

"Mmm... Delicious... What's up? You look a little worried, Tiff. Is everything alright?"

"Do I? It's fine. Well... Maybe that's not the right word but..."

"What happened? Did Brian call you drunk again? What did he want this time?" she rolls her eyes and sips more of the coffee.

"No, nothing like that. Look, I have to tell you something," I reply.

She watches me get up and close the door to her office so that no one who wanders inside the Yellow Point library can hear us by accident.

"Oh, this is serious. Ok, you have my full attention. What's the scoop? Did you finally see a ghost?" she asks and grins. Abbey loves anything to do with the paranormal and is convinced that ghosts are everywhere, we just can't see them yet because we're 'not ready.'

"Not yet! Well... Where should I start?" I tuck a strand of hair behind my ear and cradle my own cup of coffee. "You know that new professor who just moved into town to teach up at the school?"

"Sure. It feel like every single soul in Yellow Point is talking about him. The women cannot stop gushing about how handsome he is," Abbey laughs. "The men are either completely oblivious as usual, or see him as a threat, probably."

"A threat?"

"Sure. Think about it, Tiff. A very good looking and educated man who just moved here from the city. He's good with kids, dresses well, has impeccable manners from what the girls at the bakery say... he's the whole package. The men have to feel threatened by him. He's not your typical small-town guy, is he?" she explains.

"I guess not. Anyway, as it turns out, I already knew him."

Abbey gasps and her eyes widen at my piece of news.

"No way! How so?"

"He was my Literature Professor when I was a student at North Newport."

"What a small world," she says as she muses.

"Smaller than you think. I had the shock of a lifetime when he showed up on my doorstep."

"What? Why would he show up on your doorstep? And how did he know where you live?" she asks incredulously.

"As fate would have it, he moved into the house next to mine. You know, the one where old Mr. Kranston used to live. The house hasn't been kept up for a while and his shower doesn't work."

"No surprise there," Abbey replies and nods.

"Yup. So, he just knocked on my door thinking that I'm a random neighbor. To ask if he can use my shower. And, surprise, surprise, it turns out that the person behind the knock on my door is none other than Tyler Stone. Or Professor Stone as I used to refer to him. I couldn't believe it!"

"Yeah that's crazy! What did he say?"

"We spent the night having some wine and reminiscing about those college years and getting caught up on the last ten years."

"What?! You spent the evening with him? What about the shower?" Abbey asks with a smirk and a wink.

"I suppose we forgot about that," I grin.

She gives me a quizzical look but doesn't linger on the topic.

"Anyway... umm... there's something else you should know," I tell her.

"What? Do you have any other professors moving into town?" She jokes.

"That's funny. No. Tyler wasn't just my Literature professor in college."

"Ok. What does that mean?"

"Umm... well....he and I kind of had a bit of a... thing? Well, almost."

Abbey's mouth comically opens to form a perfect letter 'O' as she stares at me in shock. "You did not!! Stop! Tiffany Hart! We've been friends all these years and you never told me that you slept with any college professor!" she shrieks.

"I never slept with him! Hold on a second!" I start to laugh. "I did not say that. What I meant is that Tyler and I were very attracted to each other. From the very beginning, when I walked into his class I could see it, I could sense it. The attraction and desire were so strong that you could almost touch it. Like molasses in the air. Cloying and sticky."

"Wow, you put those literature classes to good use, didn't you? You sound like a poet talking about it," Abbey pokes fun at me.

"Maybe I was trying to impress him. And don't laugh at me, Abbey. I was in my very early twenties and here was my professor, older but very good looking, sophisticated, extremely cultured and smart. The way he talked was intoxicating. I could just sit there and listen to him for hours. I have never, in all these past years, met a man similar to or equal to him. I wanted him to like me so much."

"It looks like he did. You said that the attraction was mutual, right?" Abbey asks me, getting more and more interested in the story.

"Yes. There was no denying it. With other men in my life, I've always had to wonder. To play games. Do they truly like me? Do they want me? Or are they just dating me because they're bored or because they're attracted to me physically and nothing more. But with Tyler things were clear from the beginning. He wanted me. And he wanted me so much that it would make me squirm in my seat."

"But... how could you tell? Or did he say so to your face?"

I start to laugh as I think about those memories from long ago, memories I never thought to revisit.

"Yes. But it wasn't just that... One day, after class was over, I stayed behind. On purpose, of course. I was young, and a little crazy. Who isn't at that age? I was also in love with my own Literature Professor, so... it added to the insanity, I guess. Until then, we had only exchanged glances, stares, and small touches here and there. Professor Stone would brush his hand against mine as if by accident or he would touch my shoulder gently as he passed by my desk. Little gestures but they were enough to set me on fire. I remember just how difficult it was even to sit still in his class, if you know what I mean."

"Oh, I know what you mean!" Abbey starts to laugh. "Ethan still makes me feel like that!"

"Well, as I was saying, one day I decided that I wanted more, or to at least see what would happen. I was feeling bold and confident and found all the flirting to just be too much. What would happen if I pushed it, you know? I visited his office again towards the very end of the class. To this day, I still remember the way he touched me, slowly and intentionally, like a lion. When he ran his fingers across my lips, it was all I could do not to orgasm right then and there, standing up. We kissed and I could feel his fingers coiling in my hair, pulling me gently toward him. It was thrilling... Probably all the more exciting knowing that we could have been discovered at any point," I confess to my best friend.

"*Were* you ever discovered?" she asks, looking at me as if she's watching a particularly juicy episode of her favorite show.

"No. This was pretty much all that happened between us. Tyler put an end to everything before it was even anything. He told me that his career is very important to him. As a professor at North Newport, he was not allowed to date students. I understood and respected that. But—"

"But what?"

"The passion never went away for me. It's like... a hunger that I was never able to satiate, an itch that I was never able to scratch. Does that make any sense?"

She looks at me and nods.

"I can't say that I've ever been through *that*, but I do understand what you're telling me. So, are you going to pursue things with the fine professor now that he's reappeared in your life?"

I take a moment to think about her question and catch myself smiling just thinking about this option.

"It seems like... I was given another chance, doesn't it? Why not take it? I mean, the man is right next door to me, Abbey. Is that not a sign?"

***

The evening wraps itself around Yellow Point like a veil. I can smell the breeze coming off the sea, bringing into the house aromas from the ocean, full of seashells and sand that has been baking in the late August sun all day long. It mingles with the smell of fresh pasta and basil that has been simmering on my stove for a few minutes, creating a perfect late evening atmosphere.

I try to focus on the cooking, but my eyes keep gliding toward my phone, which is resting silently on the kitchen counter next to a glass of white wine.

Should I call him? Should I invite him over for dinner or is that too soon? Would Tyler see that as an invitation to a date or is it just something casual between old friends and new neighbors? I wish it was not so late in Paris, I'd love to call June right about now. She's not going to believe this story.

I continue to stir the pasta and the past without paying much attention to the dish as these thoughts roll around in my head. A knock on the door pulls me from my musings.

"Hello, there, neighbor!"

Tyler is at my door again, looking as glorious as ever in wet swimming trunks and a blue T-shirt.

"Oh, hey! What a surprise! I wasn't expecting to see you...but come in!"

"Wow, it smells incredible in here. You cook as well, Tiffany?" he asks and makes his way to the kitchen.

"There are a lot of things you wouldn't know about me," I reply and notice myself starting to flirt with him even though he has been in my house for less than three seconds.

I cannot keep myself from this man.

He turns and stares at me but grins.

"Is that so? Well... I suppose you will have to tell me what those other things are, then," he replies and fumbles with the wet towel in his hand.

"Have you been swimming, then?" I ask him, pointing to the towel.

"Yes, I want to make the best of the warm weather and what's left of the summer. And I keep forgetting that my shower is still not working. So..."

"Oh, I see. So that's why you're here. And I thought you were here to see me..."

He takes a few steps closer to me.

"Tiffany... I'm so—" he says cryptically.

"Yes?"

"Umm... listen, can I use your shower? I've been swimming and laying in the sand all afternoon. I'd be so grateful."

"Sure, up the stairs and to your right. You can't miss it."

As he disappears in the direction I just indicated, I am left baffled, thinking about his response. Is it possible that he doesn't feel the same way about me? Have I been misreading him?

And then, another thought strikes me. The possibility that Tyler is indeed in a relationship now and he is holding himself back.

The minutes pass slower than ever. I can hear the water running upstairs as I try to focus. Finally, I decide to put some pasta on two plates and invite him to dinner. Perhaps I can get to the bottom of this. The water stops and there is silence.

I can hear the door opening and closing above and Tyler's footsteps coming down the stairs. But, although these are typical sounds, nothing could have prepared me for what I saw next.

"Tiffany, I just realized that I haven't brought any clean clothes with me. My swimming trunks and my T-shirt are full of sand. And I don't want to put them back on. What would be the point of the shower then? Tiffany? Are you... listening?"

"Yup. Swimming trunks," I answer definitively.

I try to snap myself back into focus. Tyler is almost completely naked, covered only by the towel that he found in my bathroom. My towel. Now wrapped around this gorgeous specimen of a man. His tanned and muscular body is dripping wet, glistening in the golden evening light filtering off the sea. Around his waist, the towel is so taught that I can see the bulge of him protruding enticingly, making my head swim. All I want to do is reach out and touch him.

I lean against the kitchen counter and stare at him.

"I've known you for so long and yet, I've never seen you like this... Professor..."

He grins at my use of this word and comes forward, water dripping off his skin. With one hand, he's holding the towel and with the other he leans against the counter as well, towering over me.

"I know you've never seen me like this. But did you ever think about me like this?" he asks.

His voice is low and gravelly, seductive and intense. It makes me shiver with excitement and arousal.

"Every - single – day. I used to sit in those chairs, watching you during class and... imagine things."

"What kind of things?" he whispers back, looking at me up and down as if he's about to eat me.

"Mmm... bad things. Naughty things."

"Dirty things?" he asks me.

"You have no idea..."

"Are you still thinking them now, Tiffany?"

"I've never stopped thinking them. How could I? You are... and have always been my fantasy. The perfect dream I was not able to live. You live in my imagination, eternally..."

He groans and swallows heavily but doesn't make a move. Tyler remains still, not lowering his head to kiss me and not putting his arms around me at all.

I reach out instead and caress his taught abdomen. The tips of my fingers run across his skin lower and lower until I find the edge of the towel. I can see that he's turned on, his erection massive and bulging underneath the cotton fabric. With ease and finesse, I reach inside and tentatively touch the engorged shaft. He closes his eyes but doesn't move away. Emboldened, I move my fingers up and down. He groans.

"Oh... Tiffany. No... I can't do this... Please..."

I'm surprised at his reaction and pull my hand away.

"Is everything alright?"

He lowers his head and sighs.

"I just think I should go."

CHAPTER SIX

First Day

TYLER

"**G**ood morning and welcome to the first day of the   school year!"

The mass of students and parents gathered outside in the school's football stadium cheer as if this is a Beyonce concert and not just an ordinary day in their lives. Perhaps it isn't. I am suddenly reminded that Yellow Point is, after all, a small town and that its inhabitants lead different lives than what I am used to in the city. It's great to see so much enthusiasm for school for sure.

"Settle down, everyone, settle down!" the principal, Mrs. Walden, calls out and her voice causes the microphone to make that awful, high-pitched sound that will get dogs to howl. She's smartly dressed in a black and white dress with a red blazer, sleeves bunched up around her elbows. Her salt and pepper hair frames her face and her brightly colored yellow glasses add an interesting color pop.

Even though it's officially September, the weather has not changed. The morning sun is beating down on all of us. The locals don't seem to mind, though, another thing that reminds me I'm an outsider. I turn my attention to the principal who is just starting her speech.

"...today! So, as I was saying... Oh! There go half my notes! Well, never mind! I'll just... speak from the heart. It seems like the wind is playing a little trick on me today!" she giggles and tries not to seem even more nervous than she is.

A round of applause shows support.

"Well! Ladies and gentlemen, parents and students of Yellow Point! Welcome to your new school year! Together, we'll embark on a journey of learning, personal growth, and collaboration, ensuring every student achieves their potential and feels valued in our school community."

To my surprise, the crowd erupts into more applause and cheer as if this is the Superbowl. Wow.

She clears her throat and throws herself into the speech once more with fervor.

"As you all know, our Literature teacher, Mr. Smith has now retired. As a result, we have brought on a brand-new Literature teacher whom I am so happy to introduce. We are fortunate enough to have been selected for an important new program that enables our students to earn college credits for advanced classes, and prepare for college. Ladies and gentlemen, Mr. Tyler Stone!"

She points directly at me, and the crowd turns and stares. Mrs. Walden has not informed me that any of this would be happening.

"Come on, Mr. Stone, come up here! Let's hear what you have to say!" she yells into the microphone, a call that I am positive can be heard across the ocean.

"I don't *have* anything to say," I mumble to myself but make my way to the stage still.

"Here he is! Everyone, give him a round of applause! Mr. Stone! Our new Literature teacher!" she calls out as if I'm a new chicken at the market.

"Thank you... thank you, Mrs. Walden. I have to say, this is highly unusual."

The crowd goes silent and just looks at me. Obviously, this was not the right thing to say.

"In a good way, I mean! In a good way! It's unusual in the sense that... I have never received such a... grand welcoming before. Yes, I'm enjoying Yellow Point. You are all such lovely and warm people," I try to mend my mistake.

They seem to go for it as the crowd bursts into applause once more.

"You know, literature can have a profound impact on an individual's life, and I hope to convey the best it has to offer to all of the students. I'm reminded of what author Harper Lee said in To Kill a Mockingbird, *"Until I feared I would lose it, I never loved to read. One does not love breathing."* This essential, instinctual nature of reading is paramount to a good life I believe. I hope that we all enjoy this school year, and I am looking forward to meeting all of you. All of the children. And to teach them... literature. Umm... yes. Thank you."

I hear supportive applause and also see a few confused looks. Mrs. Walden directs me off the stage with a motherly glance.

"That's alright, you'll get the hang of it."

"The hang of what?" I ask but she's already back behind the microphone.

I quit and head toward the school. Had I known that I was going to be asked to give a speech, I would have prepared something. But... I realize that getting in Yellow Point's good books is going to be harder than I imagined.

***

"Good morning, children, and welcome to Literature class. My name is..."

"Children, Sir?"

"Excuse me?"

A boy with a mustache leans back into his chair and addresses me again.

"It's just that we're not children, Sir. Most of us are seventeen."

"Yes, of course you are. I used the word children as a way of addressing you because you are my students and because I don't know your names yet," I reply.

The young boy smirks and elbows the one sitting next to him.

"Yes. I am Tyler Stone. You can call me Mr. Stone."

"Why did you come here of all places?" a girl asks me.

"Well, as we covered in the assembly this morning to kick off the new year, I am part of the partnership program between the Yellow Point school and North Newport College. When your former teacher, Mr. Smith retired, the school applied for this program. To have a Literature professor from North Newport come here and give advanced classes for those interested in them. And to prepare you for your college admission. It was a smart move on your principal's part."

"So this class going to be really hard."

"I... suppose it will be a bit more difficult than a regular class, yes. Since this is an advanced class. You all expressed interest that you wanted to join this class, have you not?" I ask them at large.

The students look at each other and shrug.

"I don't know...."

"My mom signed me up..."

"I came because my sister said I should."

"And I have to get my grades up otherwise they won't let me go on the school trip to California at the end of the year," someone else boldly confessed.

I hesitate for a moment and realize that this class is not at all what was advertised to me when I applied. What I thought would be an advanced Literature class full of students who were eager to get ready for a good college is proving to be a group of small-town children who are only here because they have to be. If this school year is not successful, it will damage my own interest and my career advancement.

"Mmm... alright. That doesn't mean that you can't still learn. Or find a new interest in Literature that you never knew you had."

They stare blankly at me.

"Did you move here with a wife, a family?" one girl asks me. She eyes me from top to bottom, slowly and deliberately.

"I don't think that's an appropriate question for the classroom, Miss..."

"Sarah."

"What's your last name, Sarah?"

"Quinn."

"Miss Quinn."

"Why not?"

"Because we should only talk about Literature in this class, nothing else."

"Is that because you're not married? Is that why you actually came here? My mom says that you're probably divorced or that your wife died. That's why you moved to a small town like Yellow Point," Sarah Quinn continues.

I turn around for a moment, not knowing what to answer but also trying to get used to the students' blunt and free way of being.

"I am not... divorced and my wife is... There is no wife..."

"Did you kill your wife?" a boy with a mullet asks me.

"What?? Where did that come from?"

"Oh, my dad," he answers smiling. "My dad says that you might have done something and now you're in Yellow Point running from the cops."

I am honestly speechless. Something that has never happened to me before. I have been educated at Oxford, I have been teaching at North Newport College for fifteen years, and yet, I have never been speechless in this way. I have never been spoken to this way before.

"Young man, your father has been watching too many true crime documentaries. And you shouldn't believe silly conspiracy theories," I try to keep my cool. "Listen, why don't we revisit this topic later? Or... never. Now, let's open our books on page fifteen. This year, we will start with Chaucer."

"Who?"

"Foster," another one answers.

"Silence in the classroom, please! Geoffrey Chaucer was a British author who is officially referred to as "the father of English Literature or poetry.""

"Father? How many kids did he have?" says one of the kids in the back, and all the kids erupt in laughter.

This is going to be a long year.

Time seems to crawl, and when my lunch break arrives, I dart out of the school building and walk down street. All I want is to clear my head, and perhaps find the bakery that will sell me a sandwich and a glass of iced tea.

Knowing that it's almost impossible to get lost if I stay relatively close to the school, I keep walking and, no surprise at all, I reach the center of Yellow Point in only five minutes. I go inside the bakery to order.

"Hello, Tyler! You look nice today! Your suit and green tie looks very nice. Is green your favorite color? And what's your favorite movie? Do you have a…"

"Ok. Hi, Alice! Can I, please have a big glass of iced tea and a turkey sandwich? I'm on my lunch break from school and I don't have a lot of time."

"Sure! Give me just a minute!"

She starts working on my sandwich and I get a moment to breathe and relax.

"Hello, stranger! Long time, no see!"

I turn around and see Tiffany walking toward me. She's wearing a red summer dress that goes perfectly well with her tanned skin. Just the sight of her reminds me of the other night and her fingers moving expertly up and down as I grew harder and harder in her hands. I feel the beginning stages of arousal and try to focus on something else instead.

"Hi, Tiffany! How are you?"

"Great! I closed the toy shop for my lunch break and came down here to get a sandwich," she says and moves in closer to me.

I can smell a light perfume now, a combination of vanilla and flowers that works superbly well with the perpetual salt in the air.

"So will you be needing the shower again, or did yours get fixed?" she smiles and looks up at me, her bedroom eyes full of desire.

I am aware that Alice, the girl behind the counter is now staring at us. One word from this girl and the entire town of Yellow Point will be gossiping about what is happening between me and Tiffany.

"Tiffany, listen... I think we need to talk a bit about..."

"Your sandwich and tea are ready!!" Alice yells out, without a doubt, much louder than she normally would.

She's paying close attention to the conversation between me and Tiffany. I pay her, leave a more than generous tip, and invite Tiffany to come outside. We walk together down a small street that leads to a secluded beach.

"It's so beautiful here. I never imagined... mmm... this. That one day I would be able to go out for lunch on my break and simply walk to the beach. Enjoy the air, the ocean, the breeze, the sand. It's magical," I explain.

"I'm glad you like it so much, Tyler. Can I confess something to you?"

"Anything you want."

"I never imagined that you would walk back into my life. You of all people. In all honesty, I thought that chapter of my life was over and that you were nothing but a memory lost to the waves of time."

I turn to Tiffany and watch her beautiful face as she speaks. All I want is to kiss her. It would be such a perfect moment... But how can I?

"I wasn't lying the other night at my house when I told you that you have always been my perfect fantasy. Just think about it..." she confesses and blushes a little, which makes her even more beautiful. I can feel my desire for her grow and consume me. "I was a college girl, and you were my professor. The passion, the forbidden pleasure... Do you know... hmm... maybe I shouldn't tell you this..."

Not being able to resist her any longer, I put my arms around Tiffany and encourage her to speak.

"Tell me... I want to know everything. What did you dream about? What were your fantasies?" I whisper and trace my lips against her neck. She moans a little and makes me stir.

"When I watched you up there, handsome, confident, imposing. I imagined that the entire auditorium would empty on the spot so that we could..."

"So that we could what?"

She smiles and snakes her arms around my neck.

"I want to tell you a secret," she whispers. "Do you know that one day I wore a short dress and no underwear? I stood there, hoping that you would notice and that..."

"I did notice... it was all I could look at," I reply.

She lifts her head, and our lips finally meet after such a long time. I can feel her tongue sliding in, playing with mine, hypnotizing me. The kiss is consuming like fire, like the desert. My hands run all over her body and she moans, leaning more and more into me. The whole world disappears for a moment, and I get lost.

"Let's go to my house," she breathes heavily.

"What?"

"Let's go to my house... It's only five minutes away from here..." she repeats and kisses me again.

"Tiffany, I have to get back to the school. I still have classes today," I reply, even though my entire body is screaming for her. My pants are almost bursting, and my erection is painful, begging for her warmth.

"Ah of course. And I should get back to the store. If you're sure you can't miss your first afternoon of classes," she replies.

"It would be nice, for sure. It's my first day though. I should get back."

We disentangle from each other, and she rearranges her hair and her dress.

"Alright, I understand. This was fun, though... professor," she adds in the naughtiest, most delicious way possible.

I struggle to focus as she walks away, and all I can think of is undressing her and making her say that word over and over again until I spill over with pleasure.

After a few more steps, Tiffany turns around and says, "Come over when you need to... take another shower."

CHAPTER SEVEN

Candidates

TIFFANY

There is a small line in front of the toy store even though it's only nine thirty in the morning. I pass them with a smile and open the front door. A series of moms and grandmothers as well as one lost dad walk through and start to browse the shelves.

"Do you have the new Frozen puzzle? My daughter said she would like to work on it after school today."

"Yes, I want one of those too."

"How about something educational?" another mom asks with a sharp air of superiority.

"Puzzles *are* educational!" the others immediately flare up.

"Good morning all," I say in a sing-song voice. "I will take of you all this fine morning. Yes, we have a selection of puzzles that feature your favorite movies, including *Frozen*. They are in the next room. Mrs. Addelson, if you want an educational toy, how about an interactive book about the Amazon Rain Forest?"

"Yes! That will do fine! Thank you, Tiffany!"

They all look at me out of the corner of their eye as they browse through the store. I feel like an actress in a horror film, waiting for the sudden plot twist that will reveal all this clandestine curiosity. I run my fingers through my hair and check myself out in a glass window, thinking that, perhaps, I have toothpaste on my blouse or maybe just one eye of make-up completed. Did I forget to do my other eye? *Nope*. The women continue to move through the store and whisper.

"So, how are things up at the school?"

It takes me a second before I understand that the question was meant for me.

"Umm... I don't know, Mrs. Thompson. I don't have any children, as you may know."

"Yeah, I'm aware. I just thought that, maybe you have some... inside information."

"Inside information? On the school?" I ask, still trying to understand.

They look at each other and roll their eyes.

"I want to buy this one."

"The robot? Sure, Mrs. Thompson. Will that be cash or credit card?" I ask the woman as she waits for me to bag her toy.

"So... is he married?"

"Is who married?" I ask her, frozen with the credit card in midair.

She rolls her eyes again, grabs the toy and the credit card and walks out. The other customers remain in the store and continue to browse. I realize with a sudden shock that once again, word has traveled fast and some of the women in Yellow Point seem to think that Tyler and I are together, and I wonder what else about us they're assuming they know.

"Never mind them, Love. You know how they are. Once the school year starts and the kids are out of the nest, they get bored at home. Any nugget of entertainment they can get, they devour like wolves," Mrs. Robinson, my fourth grade teacher, tells me.

"I don't understand what's happening. First of all, how could they possibly know anything? And second... why do they think it's any of their business? Oh, and third – why do they care? No, Tyler is not married. So, even if I was in a relationship with him, which I'm not, what would be the problem?" I lash out, even though the old lady is on my side.

"Ugghh... it's a small town, Love. Like I said, it's a mixture of boredom, curiosity and..." she pauses and looks at me from head to toe as if she's scanning me.

"What? Am I not good enough for Tyler? Is that what they think?"

"Oh, heavens no!" the old lady starts laughing. "It's not that..."

"Then what is it? Am I not good enough for such an educated man from the city because I'm a small town girl from Yellow Point?"

"No, no. Honey, look..."

The door of the toy store opens once more and the little bell at the top chimes merrily. It distracts my attention and I look toward the source of the noise. As soon as he walks in, I let out a groan of anxiety and distress.

"What - are you doing here?!"

He raises his hands at face level as if to say that he comes in peace. I don't believe him and neither do the other women in the toy store. As always in this small town, we have an audience for everything we do.

"Tiffy, Baby, I'm just here to..."

"You may not call me that. How many times have I told you not to call me *Tiffy*? Or Baby?"

He smooths out his new goatee in what strikes me now as just....a *sleazy* gesture and comes forward toward the counter.

"I'll give you two a minute," Mrs. Robinson says as she moves two steps to her right.

"Baby, I came because I think I left some stuff at your house."

"You didn't leave anything at my house, Brian," I reply annoyed. "So you can go now."

"I did, Baby. Some... umm... shaving cream and a Kanye West CD," he answers.

I stare at him and his audacity in disbelief.

"Brian, your shaving cream is two dollars at the local supermarket. You can buy some more. And... CDs? Plea se... What is this, 1995? What do you really want, Brian?" I ask him, starting to suspect that his visit has other motives.

"Babe, look, ok, you got me. I just wanted to see you," he changes his tone to a sweet, lilting banter.

"For what?" I deadpan.

"Well, I'm... worried about you. Are you doing alright? You know... after our... breakup. I just want to know that you're ok."

I look at him incredulously, maintaining the blank expression on my face as the seconds tick by. Holding his gaze, I can only hope that he realizes the utter ridiculousness of his own question. I suddenly can not tolerate the idea of gathering the most basic unit of energy required to create a single, telling expression on my face. In this moment, as the seconds are still ticking by and I continue to stare at him blankly, it becomes crystal clear to me that using any form of communication, a core tenet of all human interaction, is simply too much of a gift for him. I simply don't have the energy for it. For him. I would like him gone now.

"Brian. I'm fine. Please, believe me when I tell you that I'm better than ever. I am not suffering in any way, shape, or form. So, go."

"But Baby... What happened between us was... brutal. How are you holding on?"

I feel like I want to smash something or throw it at his head.

"Brutal? No, Brian. It wasn't brutal. At least not for me," I answer, putting air quotes around the word *brutal*. "I found out that you were cheating on me with a random waitress, and I left you. It wasn't pleasant, but it wasn't brutal. As a matter of fact, I'm glad it happened."

"Babe, what are you talking about? You're *glad*?" he laughs. "See? This is what I mean. I don't think you're well. I think you are still suffering."

"I am not – *suffering*." I say exasperatedly, trying not to get frustrated by the conversation and the fact that the women in the store are not even pretending to shop anymore. They are watching the scene between me and Brian as if it's a tennis match.

"Baby..."

"Stop - calling – me – that!" I tell him through gritted teeth. "This. This is the reason why I'm glad you revealed your true self. Because I saw who you are, Brian! You don't respect me. You don't respect me enough even to stop calling me a pet name I never cared for, and currently serves as only a remnant of what once was. We were together for three years, and you slept with a random waitress like it was nothing! I'm happy that you're out of my life because you are simply bad news. You're an immature, selfish... man child who treated me like garbage. And now, on any other day, you're out of my life. I'm thrilled."

He stares at me with his mouth a little open like he can't comprehend the sentences I have just sent his way.

"Baby, are you jealous of Crystal?"

"Nope. I don't even know a Crystal."

"She's my new girlfriend. Because you know that you don't have to be. She and you are like... apples and pineapples. Like..."

"It's apples and oranges. And I'm happy for you Brian. Good-bye."

"Babe, I know you still love me and you're just jealous that I chose Crystal over you and..."

"You didn't choose Crystal over me," I reason, suddenly feeling like this conversation is getting the better of me. "You cheated on me with her and I immediately left you over it. Because you cheated and because you're an immature boy who..."

"Yeah? So that is why you're dating some old guy who now teaches at the school?"

Brian throws this at me. The ladies in the store gasp, taken aback by this juicy turn of events.

"What? What are you... Is that why you're here?" I feel a sense of calm wash over me all of a sudden as I understand everything.

Brian watches me in amazement as I start to laugh in his face.

"Oh, my God, Brian, is that why you came into the toy store? You heard the gossip around town that I might be dating Tyler Stone and you wanted to know if it's true? Wow... it bothers you that I moved on so fast from you to a man who is so much better, so mature, confident...just a man who is better at being an actual adult. Isn't that so?"

Brian strokes his facial hair and draws himself to his full height as if to seem much more imposing than he is.

"No! I came to see if... you're doing fine. If..." he continues to lie.

"Fine, Brian. Then yes, I am doing amazingly well, thank you. As you might have heard the word around town, am I doing... perfectly grand," I grin. "Make sure to give this message to Crystal as well, along with all my love. Tell her that if she hadn't slept with you, I would never have had the chance to be with a real man."

It's so rewarding to watch Brian's face fall in shock.

"You're fucking insane! You're... doing an old guy!" is all he can say as he walks out of the store still mumbling.

The women in the toy store are staring at me like I'm an alien.

"What else can I get for you, ladies?"

***

I know that he's home because his lights are on. It's been a week now since we kissed on the beach, and I cannot stop thinking about it. We have caught only glimpses of each other nearly every day since. We chat, wave, smile, and act civilly toward each other like the good neighbors that we are. But that magical moment on the beach has not repeated itself. Nor has Tyler asked for another shower.

On my couch, I try to focus on a random movie on Netflix. I can't pay attention as images of Tyler swim through my head. Naked, sopping wet out of the shower, hard as a rock as I touch him, kissing me...

Finally, I decide to give him a call. He answers after a short ring.

"Hey, you! How's life on the other side of the hedge?" I joke.

"Hello, Tiffany! Oh, you know... reading essays, grading papers... the usual. How about you?"

"Mmm... getting a little bored, not gonna lie."

"I see. Do you have plans to remedy that?" he asks me.

"Well, that's why I called you. I was hoping that you might have some... ideas," I reply, thankful that he can't see me smiling.

He does and to my immense relief, he starts to play along.

"I do have some... ideas, Tiffany. I've been thinking about several candidates for good ideas since the beach. And even earlier than that, to be honest. Since I came out of the shower and you... went exploring through the depths of the many folds of my towel. But honestly? I'm not sure you're ready for my ideas."

I swallow as I listen to his deep and velvety voice. My insides are melting and I'm desperate to learn more.

"No? I'm not sure you're correct on that front, Professor. I submit to you that I *am* ready, and have been in the process of becoming ready for a number of years now. I am more than prepared to entertain any cadre of potential ideas that you may be evaluating."

"Good, Tiffany, good girl."

I close my eyes and hold on to the couch when he says that. I feel an electric buzz pass through me and the pulse in my core becomes harder and almost painful.

"Mmm... do any of these potential ideas concern you coming over, Tyler. Like maybe right now?"

"Tiffany, you know the magic word," he whispers into the telephone.

"You mean 'please?' Please, come over..." I beg again, as I grind back and forth on the couch, not able to resist or wait any longer.

"No not that word. Try again."

I get a little frustrated but understand that it's part of the game.

"I don't know the magic word..."

"Then I won't come over," he replies, and I can hear him laughing a little, just as happy about this fun game as I am.

"Is that so?" it's my time to tease him. "Then too bad. Because I was going to dress like I did that day... do you remember? A short dress and no panties."

He groans into the phone, and I feel empowered and in control.

"Tiffany, what are you doing to me?"

"Fulfilling your deepest and darkest fantasies," I reply. "Won't you please come over?"

"In just one minute. Is one minute enough to put on the dress?" he asks me, hunger now in his voice.

"One minute may be too long, actually..."

Before we hang up, he tells me again.

"Tiffany, say the magic word."

I hesitate with the phone still in my hand.

"*Professor...*"

CHAPTER EIGHT

Cadre of Ideas

TYLER

I slip the phone in my pocket and rush into the kitchen to find a bottle of wine. My head is so dizzy and my desire so insatiable that I can hardly believe this is happening. I can feel my heart beating so fast that it threatens to leave me out of breath. I stop for a moment to check the way I look in the hallway mirror but also to

c   h   e   c   k

m   y   -

self.

The moment that I have been waiting for so long, the fantasy that I have been keeping all these years to myself is about to come to fruition in only a few minutes. Real life seems nothing but a wisp now, a layer of film or paint on a canvas.

I shut the door behind me and rush across the lawn to her house. With the bottle of wine in my hand, I knock a little too loudly in my excitement.

"Come in..." I hear her say.

I open the door and am met with an enchanting view. I have no idea how she accomplished all of this in the couple of minutes since our call. Tiffany's living room is bathed in the dim and blueish fading light of the night, pierced here and there by golden candles. It smells sweetly of perfume and roses, beckoning an evening full of sensuality and intimacy.

She's sitting on a chair at the living room table and doesn't get up to greet me. I close the front door and advance slowly into the beautifully set living room.

"This is... you look incredible," I tell her as I notice that she is, indeed, wearing a very short dress. It's black and loose fitted, the glossy silk flowing over her bare breasts and thighs like water.

"Come on in, Professor," she says and looks me in the eyes, almost defiantly.

I place the bottle of wine on the coffee table and come closer to her.

"Stay there," she says, which takes me by surprise a little.

"Here?"

"Mhm..."

"Why?"

"Oh, just because... I thought this would be... fitting. I'm recreating that day. Our small but incredible fantasy. You at the podium, holding your lecture. And me in my seat, squirming, hoping you would notice me."

"I did notice you, Tiffany. When you wore that dress, it was all I could think of."

"But you didn't do anything about it..."

"How could I? We were surrounded by so many peop le..." I reply and watch her elegant, cat-like movements.

"Well, maybe you will do something about it now."

As she's sitting in the chair in front of me, she pulls the shiny, black dress up her thighs until I can see the heavenly triangle between her legs. The way the watery fabric travels across her skin makes me shiver. And then, slowly and deliberately, Tiffany opens her legs and lets me see the full spectacle that is happening there.

"Glad you and your cadre of ideas could make it. I have a couple of my own, you know, Professor..." she says, and my eyes are now fixed on that spot.

Her legs now open wide, she lowers her hands to the soft triangle and starts touching herself. With her fingers, she opens the petals and gives me a full view of everything that waits for me inside. I move painfully from one leg to the other as the show she's putting on for me is by far the most erotic thing I have ever seen in my entire life.

Not wasting a single moment, she runs the tips of her fingers up and down the pink petals, hesitating at the top, where her point of pleasure is. She rubs her clitoris with her fingers, circling it again and again in a mad game, causing herself so much pleasure and me so much pain that I can barely stand it.

I can see her slick wetness move slowly from her opening and gather on the chair.

"Please..." I beg her, my thirst beyond anything I felt in my life. "Please..."

She nods, wanting me to approach. I cross the distance between us in two steps and fall to my knees in front of her and that heavenly display. With her fingers, she opens the petals even more, and I dive in, my lips and my tongue enjoying the sensation of impossibly slick, soft skin and the exquisite taste of her. She allows her head to fall back as I run my tongue across her clitoris. I can't help myself anymore and I feast on it, taking the tiny mound of pleasure into my mouth and enjoying it like the sweetest candy ever created. I suck it lightly and can hear Tiffany moaning louder and louder.

"Oh, God... Mmm... My God... Don't stop..."

I would never... There is nothing on the face of the planet that could make me stop right now. I run my tongue across her opening, all the way from the top of the engorged clitoris to the bottom as she uses her fingers to open it more and more for me. I want her so much now that I feel like a wild animal. A deep and intense desire that I have never felt for another woman is taking control of me.

She starts to cry out and move back and forth, rubbing her swollen clitoris against my tongue.

"Mmm... Oh, God! Oh, God! Yes!! Yes!!"

She screams and lets go, her eyes closed tightly against the light and the world, her entire body contracting, her clitoris pulsating in my mouth. I hold her in place and watch as she enjoys this shattering orgasm. It makes me feel powerful. Like a King. Knowing that I have been able to do this. To create this ocean of pleasure in this woman makes me feel like a titan.

I continue to kiss her gently as I run my tongue across her opening, giving her the aftercare that she needs after such an orgasm. Finally, after several moments, she lifts her head and opens her eyes, smiling from ear to ear.

"Mmm... that feels so good..." she says and watches me take care of her softest and most intimate part.

"Are you ready for more?" I ask, getting to my feet.

My erection is throbbing in my pants, and she casts it a glance.

"More? Oh... more... Yes, yes, I am."

"Say that magic word," I command.

"Come here, *Professor*..."

"Too late," I tell her half-jokingly. "How many times have I told you to say the magic word? And you simply refuse. Tell me, Tiffany, do you want to fail this class?"

"Of course, not, Professor," she grins, playing along. "I would do anything not to fail your class. It's much too important for me."

"Anything? I'm glad to hear that. But first I will have to discipline you. Stand up."

"Discipline me?" she asks as she playfully stands up and looks into my face.

"Yes. You've been such a bad girl, Tiffany. Such a bad girl..."

I direct her toward the couch and ask her to face the wall. I grab her hands and place them on the wall in front of her. As she does so, her black dress lifts up a little and exposes her backside. My erection is now throbbing and painful, but the game is far too enticing.

"Are you going to spank me, Professor?" she asks in a whisper and turns her head toward me a little.

"Are you a bad girl?"

"Such a bad girl..."

I lift the hem of her dress and her full and round cheeks come into view. As I run my hands across them, I can see her starting to shiver in anticipation. I understand this feeling all too well as I am ready to burst myself. But the fantasy we are finally bringing to life is far too good to end now.

She's still so wet from my touch and the anticipation of the pleasure that is about to come. I run my thumb across her opening, and she moans loudly, letting me know just how much she enjoys it. I linger with my finger at the opening, teasing my entrance. She stops breathing for a moment, waiting for the exquisite pleasure but I deny it.

"You're a bad girl..."

"Please... please," she begs me and it's the sweetest sound I've ever heard. My erection stirs on its own in my pants, and I have to undo my zipper to make myself more comfortable.

"No... not until you learn how to behave..."

I lift my hand and let it fall across her perfect behind. She gasps loudly as the touch of my palm against her skin makes a satisfying noise.

"Mmm... God..." is all she manages to say.

"No. That's not the magic word."

"Professor..."

I lift my hand again and let it fall once more across the same cheek. She twitches and moans heavily. Her head falls forward across her chest, and she closes her eyes to enjoy the sensation.

I indulge her and allow a couple more satisfying smacks, and then run my hands over body, embracing her completely and attempting to fully realize the thrill of her being in my arms. She is so wet now that it's dripping down the insides of her thighs. I slip my hand in between her legs and drag my fingers across her slit. It's dripping wet, hot, slick and clearly ready for more. When I reach the opening, I hesitate there, still wanting to tease her. But she can't wait any longer. Tiffany pushes back against my hand, and I pull back and watch as my finger glides inside her easily and smoothly, covered in her heavenly oil.

She moves back and forth a few times, satisfying herself against my hand before I put a stop to it and leave her wanting more.

"No... please... please... more..." she begs.

"Mmm... of course... if that's what you want, favorite student..." I growl in her ear.

I pull her up and against me. In one, quick and effortless move, I pull down the straps of her glossy black dress. Her naked breasts pop up, full and round, the nipples hard against my hands.

"Do you have any kind of idea how many times I've fantasized about you like this?" I ask her.

"No..." she whispers.

I know that she can't focus anymore, the pleasure too high, and the anticipation almost too much. Her breath is labored and as she struggles to keep it under control, her breasts move up and down, enticing me. I take each nipple in between my fingers and start to roll it and pull at it gently. She gives out a loud moan as I stretch her nipples in between my fingers. Her body is now a perfect S, her backside glued to me and begging to be taken, her breasts pushed inside my hands and wanting as much attention as possible.

The time has come. I cannot control myself any longer. As much as I love the game between us, the fantasy that we have managed to bring to fruition after so many years, I cannot wait anymore. Still rolling her nipples and teasing them roughly, I pull her down a little until her backside is exposed again.

I take a deep breath and direct my shaft toward her. Slowly, I push the engorged head through the lips and can hear her moaning already. But it's a distant sound as if coming from another room. My own head feels as if it's filled with cotton. All I can concentrate on is just how intense the pleasure is and trying to squeeze every exquisite moment out of it.

Deliberately, I drive the entire length of the shaft as slowly as possible inside her until she is supremely full. The sensation is beyond words. I can feel her pulsating around me, warm and tender, like the happiest place I've ever been. She's eager and hungry, so she starts to move back and forth, pleasuring herself on my long and hard shaft. I allow her to do as she pleases, the rhythm intoxicating my brain. I can see her incredible body contort and move up and down as she takes every inch of me, more and more until she screams and holds it in, enjoying the pleasure.

She backs fully into me now, closer than we've ever been, and allows her head to fall on my shoulder. I lower one of my hands from her nipples to her clitoris. As expected, it's drenched in juices, which I find intoxicating. I circle it with my thumb, rubbing it harder and harder as I continue to pull at her nipples and go in and out of her from behind. Her points of pleasure pleased to the extreme, Tiffany tries to control her moaning. With my eyes barely open, I can see her trying to cover her mouth with her hand, but it doesn't work. She holds on tightly to me and opens her legs even more, allowing me full access. Swollen and pulsating, her clitoris is surrendering itself to me for more and more pleasure.

I continue to move in and out of her in a maddening rhythm that carries me away. After I close my eyes, I have no more notion of time or space. Just Tiffany's body, all those points of pleasure that are mine now, and her loud moaning that turns into screams. I can feel her climaxing all around me. Her nipples become hard as diamonds, and she squeezes my shaft for every ounce of pleasure she can get.

We hold on to each other and let go at the same time, carried over by the immensity of the whole experience, moving in unison and pleasuring each other.

She turns around and collapses into my arms, spent and exhausted. I direct her softly toward the couch and we remain there, coiled in each other. She wraps herself around me and places one of her long and gorgeous legs around my waist as we sit on the couch, catching our breath. I continue to kiss and caress her, making sure that she gets all the after play she deserves. My fingers travel down her back and find her soft petals once more. I start to rub them gently and caringly, nurturing them after our session of lovemaking. She lets out a sigh of satisfaction and pushes herself further into my hand, like a cat that wants attention. I continue to stroke her petals with my fingers, caressing them back down, until I can feel her relaxing and almost falling asleep.

"Mmm... don't stop... that feels so good..." she says, half asleep now in my arms.

"Never."

Her head is on my chest and her arms are wrapped around me. I am enveloped by a feeling of bliss and satisfaction such that I have never felt in my entire life. I have always dreamed of Tiffany and wondered whether I should find search her out after her college years. Now, sitting here with her after our incredible love making, I curse myself silently for not doing so.

Why did I miss out on all those years of pure bliss? She's right. This has always been my fantasy, my dream, my secret desire. The one thing I could never get out of my head, no matter what. The one woman I could never forget or get over. Time was not able to erase her from my mind or from my body. Other women have been pale comparisons to her. Nothing has been able to erase her from me, tightly tied in to my very existence.

And it feels that it never will.

CHAPTER NINE

Breakfast

TIFFANY

I open my eyes against the pale sun that filters through the window. Memories of last night flood my mind instantly, and I feel a gigantic smile blossom on my face. I turn around in bed and stretch out my arm, looking for Tyler. The bed is empty, and I get up on one elbow to l   o   o   k around.

"Tyler?" I call out, hoping he hasn't left my house before I woke up. "Tyler, are you still here or…"

A second of panic courses through my body until I hear his voice coming from the kitchen.

"In here! I'm making breakfast. Come on in!"

I leap out of bed, pull on an old T-shirt that has been hanging on the back of a chair, and charge down the stairs. In the kitchen, the man of my dreams is cooking a delicious smelling omelet that makes my belly rumble.

"Wow... you are the perfect man; do you know that?" I ask and hug him from behind.

I watch as he turns the omelet expertly, the golden eggs coming together as if by magic under his strong hands.

"The perfect man? I don't know about that..."

"Come on... last night you... set fireworks inside me and now, here you are, making me breakfast. I mean... you're almost too good to be true," I reply and kiss him.

He turns around and smiles.

"You haven't tasted the eggs yet."

He hands me a plate and we sit down at the round table in my kitchen. Tyler pours me a cup of coffee but doesn't say much else.

"Is... everything alright? You're awfully quiet."

"Hmmm? What? No... I was just thinking about my day, that's all," he replies.

"Hard day at school coming up today?"

"Something like that," he says.

"How are things going over there?"

"Well... I have to confess, it's not exactly what I imagined it to be," he replies and, by the look on his face, I can tell that this is much more serious that I thought.

"What do you mean? Are people giving you a hard time because you're not from Yellow Point?"

"No, no. To be honest, when I came from the city, I thought that the program would be, well, what was advertised to me."

"And what was that?" I ask, finishing up my eggs.

"Small town kids who were very dedicated and who needed someone to tutor them so that they have a better chance of applying to a good college. I saw this as a wonderful opportunity to help the students who might, otherwise, not have the same chances as the others."

I nod and smile.

"That was an amazing thing on your part, Tyler. I love how dedicated you are to your job. And to the students."

"But that's not exactly what I found here. Most of the students are taking the classes because they have to or because they're parents told them to. I don't know... I hope I'm not wasting my time," he confesses and puts down his fork.

"Come on, don't say that. Wasting your time? What about me?" I ask, munching on my avocado toast.

I reach out across the table and caress the back of his hand. His fingers snake through mine and he holds my gaze for a moment.

"Yes, of course. That's not what I meant. Maybe..."

"What?"

"Never mind. Did you enjoy your breakfast?"

I am a little taken aback by the sudden change of topic, but I nod, nonetheless. I felt as if this conversation in which Tyler was expressing his innermost feelings to me had brought us closer. However, all of a sudden, he chooses to change the subject.

"I loved every bit of it! You're a great chef!" I compliment him.

"I'm glad you loved it."

He gets up, kisses me, and heads for the door.

"I have to go. My first class is in about half an hour, and I don't want to be late. Shall we talk later, though?" he says in his usual, classy manner. "And Tiffany. Last night was amazing."

"You bet, and yes, it was!"

A moment later, he's gone. I clean up the remains of the breakfast we just shared and feel myself soaring. An incredible night with the man of my dreams that could not have ended better.

***

"Hey, are you ready for lunch?" Abbey walks through the door of the toy store, making the little bell ring. I look up and feel confused for a moment.

"Oh, God. Is it already lunch time? I hadn't even noticed."

"It's past lunch time, actually. I had to stay longer at the library, thanks to your crush. Or old college crush. Umm... Professor Stone," she says in a teasing tone. "He has been setting all sorts of essays and reading tasks for the kids, and now they're in and out of the library all day long."

"That's a good thing, isn't it? And, please, don't call him my crush, Abbey. Or my college crush."

"But he is... your college crush," she continues to grin.

I turn around to look for my purse, thinking that, in the meantime, Tyler has become much more than that. Abbey catches the grin on my face.

"Hold on a second! What are you... What's that smile all about? Oh, Tiffany. Have you been a bad girl?" she laughs.

"Umm... it depends on what you mean by bad. Because let me tell you – it was good. Exceptionally good!"

We both burst out laughing, catching the innuendo.

"No way! You slept with him?? You slept with Tyler Stone? Your old college professor," she keeps asking as if I've done something so out of the ordinary that no one could have imagined.

"Jeez, Abbey, it's not like I discovered the cure for cancer," I laugh and roll my eyes. "Come on, let's go to lunch. I'm starving."

We step out onto the sidewalk and are met by a gust of cold wind. The smell of the ocean changes in autumn to a steel and salt smell that rubs onto your skin. All around us, the streets of Yellow Point are almost deserted, most children being in school and most adults being at work.

Abbey crosses her arms to protect herself against the wind, and we start walking down the street toward Jake's restaurant.

"Come on, come on! Why are you grilling me like this? I need to know all the details, and I need to know them now!" she laughs.

"God, fine... I guess it just happened."

"Yeah, right. Tiff, these things don't just happen. You don't just sleep with your old literature professor by accident. This is not a Hallmark movie! Come on, tell me. Who initiated it? Was it him or was it you?"

We take a few more steps while I gather my thoughts. But we're already in front of Jake's, and I hesitate to go in, not knowing if it's private enough to have this conversation with my best friend.

"Well, we kind of, sort of, already kissed about a week ago," I confess.

"What??" Abbey explodes.

"Shhh... Abbey, please. I don't want to make a huge deal out of this."

"But it is a huge deal, Tiff!"

"No, it's not. Look, people just think it is because this is Yellow Point and because Tyler has just moved here. But if it were anyone else, any other man here, no one would even care what we did."

"Sure, but there's also... the other thing," Abbey says.

"What other thing?"

"You know, the fact that he's twenty-one years older than you. That counts for something, especially here, in Yellow Point," she says wisely.

"Come on, let's go inside and get some burgers or whatever," I reply, trying to delay this side of the conversation as much as possible.

A few minutes later, we emerge from Jake's with our sodas, burgers and fries, packaged up to go. Even though it's getting chilly outside, and our hands are turning red with the wind, we decide that it's much better to find a quiet bench in the small park that overlooks the ocean than to deal with the crowd at Jake's.

"Here comes winter," she says and sips her Dr. Pepper.

"Yeah, I know…"

"Anyway, enough small talk. So, what happened? You kissed about a week ago and then what?"

"And then, nothing. We kept bumping into each other as usual, saying hello, and flirting like mad. But he didn't make a move. So, last night I called him."

"Get out of here! You called him? Just like that? I would never have the courage even to pick up the phone!" she laughs.

"Yeah, I know. Normally, me neither. But... there's just something about Tyler. The idea that he has returned to my life so out of the blue. That the man of my dreams is right next door and that I could get to live the fantasy I have been thinking about for so long... I think it made me forget about everything else and just call him."

Abbey is staring at me with her mouth open as if she's watching an episode of her favorite TV show.

"Wow... I'm living vicariously through you right now," she says. "And then what? How did you get him to come over? Did you invite him to dinner or something?"

"That was the plan. But, as soon as he picked up the phone we just started flirting. Heavily, I might add."

"So that means that he was thinking about it as well!" Abbey exclaims as if she's just uncovered the clue to a mystery.

"Yes, I believe so. It gave me a lot of courage. It was kind of understood between us that he would come over and... he did. And then we... did it," I reply, trying to sound as casual as possible.

"God, just imagine. Being able to make your biggest fantasy come to life with just one phone call," Abbey muses. "What must that be like? I mean, I made my own come true by just showing up at abandoned properties until I ran into Ethan, but that was different."

"Maybe. It is mind-blowing. I mean, here is this incredible man that I have been dreaming about since college. Even back then I was in love with him. And I already told you about our kiss and how he refused to go any further."

"Because of the college's policies."

"Yeah... But now, there is nothing standing in our way, Abbey. We are both free, grown up, and ready to do whatever we want. I guess what I'm trying to say is that I feel as if life has given me one more shot, you know? Fine, I know this sounds corny as hell. But think about it. Doesn't this seem like our chance to live what we should have lived all those years ago?"

Abbey sips her drink before answering me.

"Do you think you can live like that in Yellow Point?" she asks.

"Why not? Who would stop us?"

"It's not that people would stop you, Tiff. It's just that... this is a very small town, and a traditional one at that. People here are not that thrilled about this kind of stuff. You and I, sure, we're excited for college fantasies, steamy romances with foreign men who sweep us off our feet, and all that. But everyone else..."

I take another bite of my delicious cheeseburger and ponder her words.

"So, what are you trying to say, Abbey?"

"Just that people might take issue with the fact that he's so much older than you. And a teacher up at the school, that's all."

"First of all, we don't know if people will react like that. And second of all, why do you think that I would even care about something like this?"

"You don't care but Tyler might."

Her words hit me like a ton of bricks. For some reason that I can't quite put my finger on, the conversation begins to irk me all of a sudden.

"I don't get it. Why are you against this? Why are you against me?" I ask Abbey.

She freezes with the burger lifted halfway up to her mouth, her eyes wide as she stares at me, no doubt having been taken by surprise by my question.

"Tiff... I'm not against this or against you. Why would I be?"

"That's exactly what I'm asking!"

"Okay, I think you got this backwards. Look, I was only pointing out pretty much the obvious. I'm sorry if that offended you, but I didn't mean it like that, Tiff."

"But that's the whole thing! How do you know that this is the obvious? Why are you so certain that people will be against us?"

"Tiffany, I think you need to calm down. I did not say that I'm certain. Just that there is a possibility of this happening because we live in such a small town that is not used to outsiders or to big age gap relationships," she explains.

"I get that! But why should this be a problem for Tyler, then?" I refuse to back down, even though, in my heart, I know that she's right.

"It shouldn't! Tiff, this was just a thought I had. I'm sorry it bothered you so much," she replies and stands up.

Abbey throws the rest of the burger in the trash and begins to walk away.

"Look, I have to go back to the library. Maybe we can talk later or something?"

I can see that she's annoyed. With me or the conversation, I don't know.

"Abbey, I'm sorry, I didn't mean to lash out," I call after her. "Listen, I think I reacted like this because... Well, because Tyler has already rejected me once. Back then, for mostly the same reasons. And then we were apart for ten years. And then there's the Brian situation, as well. No matter how much I try to pretend that I'm fine, I cannot deny the fact that it hurt me. What he did, cheating on me with a random waitress he met at a bar? I felt as if I was getting... as if I was getting rejected all over again. I guess this conversation triggered me."

She puts her arms around me and sighs.

Alright, don't worry about it. I understand. And, you know what? Tyler is a much better man than Brian could ever be. Not only that, but you're right. You are not in college anymore and he's not your professor. Yes, things will work out this time," she smiles and makes me feel reassured.

"That's precisely what I was saying..." I add and smile.

We part ways a moment later, and I watch her walk away toward the library. I pull my coat closer to my body and head in the opposite direction.

Yes, things have to work out this time.

CHAPTER TEN

Beach

TYLER

The weekend drew in rapidly, bringing with it some much needed sun. I sip the last dregs of coffee and try to focus on the essays in front of me. I have been reading and grading them the entire morning, but secretly wishing I could spend my Saturday on the beach, enjoying the ocean, the sand and, of course, Tiffany. Still, my work has to come first.

Romeo and Juliet's relationship is kind of toxic. And I didn't really get why they had to unalive themselves. I mean, they should have gone to therapy to work on their relationship. Also, where do you even get poison? I'm not asking for me, I'm just saying.

I continue to read the essay written by a girl in one of my classes on Shakespeare's play. I am taken aback by the grammatically incorrect word she uses to describe the famous couple's actions. But, after a quick Google search, I find out that it's a social media term. Literature essays written using popular social media terms like *unalive*. Fantastic.

This play is kind of... I don't know. Because I saw the play Cats two years ago when my parents took me, and I liked the singing. This is kind of boring. Except for at the end when they die. That was at least interesting.

Another essay, this time written by a boy, has me wondering if I should approach my classes a different way. And if this boy is somehow psychologically challenged.

I try to take another sip of coffee but realize that my cup is empty. The autumn sun keeps shining through my windows as if inviting me, begging me to go outside. It's actually a warm-ish afternoon and the open skies and rolling ocean continue to demand my presence outdoors.

Overlooking the essays that I still have not read or graded, I reach for my phone.

"Well hello, Professor!"

Her voice is bright and sunny, like the weather. My heart skips a beat and I can't help smiling, almost foolishly, like a teenager caught in a summer romance.

"Hi, Tyler! So happy to hear from you! What's up?"

"Nothing much. Grading essays, as usual. And thinking of you. As usual."

I can hear the pleasure in her voice when she speaks again. "Hmm... is that true? Or are you just trying to flirt with me, Professor?" I can practically see her grinning ear to ear.

"Why can't it be both? Because I am one hundred percent trying to flirt with you. Is it working?"

"You have no idea..."

"Then here's a thought – what do you say we go down to the beach? I can pack up some lunch for us, take a blanket or two and we can spend the rest of the afternoon there."

She squeals into the telephone.

"I knew it! I knew you were perfect! Yes. How long do you need to get all this ready? And should I bring something as well?"

"About half an hour. And you don't have to bring anything. Just yourself," I reply.

"Nothing?" She continues to flirt with me. "Not even a bathing suit?"

"It's October. I don't think you'll need a bathing suit," I say, playing right into her hands.

"Well, then, I won't wear one. I won't be wearing anything at all... underneath..." she adds in a sultry voice.

Images of her perfect, naked body start to swim through my head. Her baiting words succeed, and I can barely wait to see her, especially since I know the surprise she is preparing for me.

"Tiffany... is it possible that I'm the luckiest man in the world?"

"Let's meet in half an hour, and you'll find out!" she laughs.

Not a minute later than half an hour, we meet on the tiny beach behind our houses. I'm already there, having come earlier to set up the picnic in front of the berm, shielding us from the possibility of any wandering eyes belonging to other neighbors. I can see Tiffany coming down the sandy pathway. She's wearing a long, blue dress that covers her entirely but at the same time, is snug and I can see all her gorgeous curves as she walks toward me. A soft, black sweater hangs loosely and romantically across her bare shoulders, and I cannot peel my eyes off this gorgeous woman.

"You look like a painting. Like an ethereal music video. Like a muse, weaving nothing but beauty and joy into the fabric of my day."

She laughs, her beautiful face illuminated by the rays bouncing off the face of the water. In a fluid, swift motion, almost like a cat, she bends down onto the blanket and deposits herself directly in my lap. Her arms link around my neck and, breathlessly, she kisses me deeply.

"Mmm... I adore the fact that you're a literature professor. Who else would pay me these kind of compliments?"

I continue to kiss her face, her neck and her arms, trying to reach every inch of bare skin I can find. She smells like vanilla and dark cherries, an intoxicating aroma that fills my very soul.

"And I love that you're... you!" I reply, sliding my fingers underneath her sweater.

Behind us, the sun is well on its way to setting, bathing the entire beach in tones of gold, orange, and fiery pink.

The view is stunning, but it does not compare to how beautiful Tiffany is.

I can feel her moving slightly in my lap as she's getting more and more aroused by our kissing and touching.

"I missed you so much," she says, not opening her eyes and not stopping even for a second. Her lips meet my lips, her tongue caresses mine, and her hips sway back and forth, causing my desire to escalate.

"How much?" I ask her, aware that my voice has become husky, the desire for her awakening something primal and animalistic in me.

"This much."

She takes off her black sweater and throws it to the side. The blue dress clings to her body like the whisper of a summer breeze and I can see her nipples now, hard and aroused, and a hunger takes over me.

"It's getting cold, my darling. I don't want you to be too chilled," I tell her.

"Believe me, I'm not. But if you really don't want me to be cold, your touch will most likely save me from the effect of any further dipping of the temperature," she teases me.

I watch in awe as she reaches for the thin straps of the blue dress with her own hands and pulls them down. Her breasts bounce out and toward me, tempting me like the sweetest fruit that has ever existed. In the middle, rosy nipples beg for my attention as Tiffany arches her back and pushes them forward.

My head is heavy with desire and my groin is starting to grow. I lean my head down and find one of her nipples with my lips. She moans as my tongue circles it again and again, causing it to harden and build. Gently, I take the nipple in my mouth and start sucking at it. She responds immediately and allows her head to tilt back, her eyes closed as if to intensify the sensation. I bite her nipple softly, making her squirm.

"Oh, God! Oh... my God..."

The words, as few as they are, fill me with joy. Being able to cause so much pleasure in this woman gives me more satisfaction that I've ever felt. My hands are locked firmly on her hips. I pull up the dress, almost tear at it with my bear hands, my own urges taking the best of me. The dress goes over her hips, and I realize that she kept her word. There is not a single trace of underwear, just her incredible hips and backside swaying in my lap.

"You're such a good girl, Tiffany. Good girl..."

I can hear her sharp intake of air as I say those words, and I know they have the magical effect I was hoping for. I reach around her hip, caress the creamy skin of her behind, and allow my fingers to dance along her opening. Her slippery fluid covers my fingers in an instant, letting me know of her immense desire. I slip in so easily, my fingers feeling the warmth and tightness of her intimacy.

"Aaah... Please... Mmm... please," she begs.

"What? What do you want? Tell me."

Her eyes are still closed as she tries to handle the intense pleasure radiating from within. Holding tightly to my shoulders, I can feel her grinding back and forth against my fingers, against my hand, giving herself all the delight and satisfaction that she craves. I dip further inside her, making her squirm and shake. Her body is trembling, and her hands dig into my shoulders. She's close now, I know it. I can feel her pulsating around my slippery fingers.

"I want... you... So much... You!! You...!!" she screams as I continue to run my fingers in and out of her.

But, all of a sudden, she opens her eyes and stares at me.

"Why did you stop?" she asks, confused and still trembling.

"Because I want you just as much..." I reply.

She understands what I mean and grins. Her legs wrap around me in an instant and she positions herself better. I am so aroused now that it's almost painful. But, only a moment later, I watch as she lowers herself onto me. I disappear inside her, smooth and slick, inch by inch until the whole of me fills the whole of her. Still holding onto my shoulders, she leans back, and I can see her entire, almost naked body in all of its glory.

Her breasts, the nipples long and aroused, poke the air as she moves up and down on me. My hands grab her waist, and I support her in this mad choreography of pleasure. My eyes glide down the length of her body. It's immensely erotic to see myself appear and disappear as she moves, to hear her loud moans, the very moans that I am causing within her.

The stretched petals of her intimacy reveal her engorged and swollen clitoris. It's begging for my attention, and I oblige. With my thumb, I start to circle it, feeling its rigid softness against the tip of my finger. Tiffany's scream echoes on the empty beach when I make contact with her clitoris. She grabs me even harder and starts to move wildly, her hips bucking in my lap. It's as if I'm trying to hold on to water now.

Her legs open wide, and I can see that incredible show, the intensely erotic center of her, the most spectacular thing I have ever seen in my life, burned into my brain.

"More! More!" she says. A seagull, somewhere across the vastness of the ocean seems to echo her.

She shifts a little and I can feel heaven. The rhythm becomes quicker, and her pulsations drive me wild. I hold on to her hips and lose touch with reality for a moment as the orgasm takes over me, hard and crashing, like a tornado. I can hear Tiffany let out similar moans to mine, a sign that she too is experiencing the same bliss.

I float in an ocean of pleasure before I can manage to open my eyes again. She is still move slightly on top of me, spent but satiated, a look of deep satisfaction on her face.

"You're incredible... I've never felt anything like this before. I didn't even know it could be like this," I confess, and I am not lying.

Out of all the women in my life, none have been this erotic, this open, and this magnificent. She is simply outstanding, and I crave more.

"Mmm... shall I tell you how I feel, professor?"

"You better. Or else many points will be deducted."

The sexy game continues between us, enticing and tingling. I want to play this game forever.

"I feel like I'm dreaming. Like none of this is real. Like... I was in love with you in college and then, ten years later, I managed to dream you into life."

"It's not a dream. I'm right here. But you are a fantasy, Tiffany," I reply as we start kissing again.

***

The only lights on the beach are the ones that shine dimly above us, from the row of houses on the street. My house as well as Tiffany's is shrouded in darkness, but the others are merrily lit, as if just for us. After the intense lovemaking we shared, the picnic is well underway now. She bites hungrily into the chicken salad while I pour some white wine.

"Mmm... this is delicious. I've had chicken salad a million times before, but it's never tasted so good," she smiles. "You, know, I think it's because of you!"

"I think it might be all the... exercise we did a few minutes ago," I reply, trying to remain modest but still enjoying her compliment above all.

"Exercise? That was a marathon! And I loved every second of it!" she leans in and kisses me.

The waves crash sleepily just a few feet away from us but, thankfully, the wind is not picking up at all. The night has remained pleasant and comfortable enough for us to have dinner on the beach without freezing over. I can smell the brine of the ocean settling in my skin and I enjoy the peace it brings.

"What's up?" she asks me. "You look... what's the word? Is it pensive?"

"Yes, that's the correct word. Maybe I am a little pensive."

"What's up? Is it the school?"

"In a way," I reply and drink some white wine. It's crisp and sweet, perfect for this evening. "Tiffany, I have to tell you something."

"Is it about how good I am at... that? Did I get an A, professor?" she grins.

"An A plus, in fact. Because yes, you are my star student," I reply and kiss her.

"What's up?" she purrs like a contended kitten.

"Tiffany, we need to talk about something. Namely, my position at the school."

She catches up on my suddenly serious demeanor.

"I'm listening."

"So, I came here from North Newport College, as you well know as a replacement for AP classes. For Literature. This is a pilot program, the first of its kind, that the college has initiated in partnership with the school here in Yellow Point. It's a wonderful opportunity for both me and the students."

"Yeah, I kind of knew all that already," she replies.

"Of course. But what you may not have known is that the project is only meant to last one year."

She stops moving and stares at me. Even her eyes have ceased to blink now, that's how intensely she's gazing at me, as if she could scan me and read my mind.

"What... what are you trying to tell me, Tyler?" she asks.

"I'm not trying to tell you anything. Just this," I reply.

"Just... this?? Just – the fact that you're only here for one year. That's all. Oh... Umm... How come you didn't tell me this sooner?"

"I didn't think this was secret information. The parents and the school know this. But, lately, I've gotten the feeling that you might not be aware of this. Also, seeing as things are progressing between us, I thought it might be a good idea to talk about it."

"Did you??" she slams down the glass. It makes a soft thud in the sand. "Tyler... so... so what are you saying? That once this school year is over you will leave Yellow Point?"

"Yes."

"Just... just like that?"

"Not just like that. Tiffany, that's exactly why I wanted to talk to you. When I accepted to be part of this project and come here, I had no clue I was going to find you in Yellow Point. You of all people. How could I have known? I mean, sure you talked up Yellow Point so much all those years ago, but I had no inkling I'd actually find you here, next door no less. But I did and this thing between us is progressing beyond anything I could have ever imagined. As a result, we need to figure out our next move."

She looks around into the empty night, but there is nothing there. Only a few stars above and the white froth of the waves close by.

"Alright. Well, then, it's logical that you would just stay beyond this year. What's so difficult? There, I solved it!" she says.

"I'm afraid it's not that simple. When the project is over, I have to return to Newport and to my job, of course. The school here in Yellow Point has no confirmation of means to hire me further. So, I have to go back. Plus, I have my career, my book..."

Tiffany rubs her forehead with her fingers.

"I see. So, all of those things are more important than me?" she asks.

"That's not what I said. This is just what I have to do. Think about it, Tiffany. What would I do in Yellow Point?"

"Be with me?"

Her voice breaks and she turns her head, not wanting me to see tears that are forming in her eyes. The situation is sadder than I could have imagined, so I try to reach out for her, but she pushes my hands away.

"Tiffany, please. You're taking this far more personal than you should. This has nothing to do with you. But with the fact that I simply must return to my job and my career."

"Except that you don't! Except that you could just stay here, with me, and work on your book. Give private lessons, tutor children. There are a million things you could do, but... you just don't want to stay here..."

"You know that's not true. And the fact that you have this opinion of me hurts me, Tiffany. Why don't you move to the city with me?"

"What? And leave the toy store? How could I do that?"

"Then you understand what it's like," I reply and smile bitterly.

"Understand? What is there to understand?"

"That we are in the same situation. I can't remain in Yellow Point and you can't leave it."

She looks at me with desperation in her face.

"So... this is all just a... fling."

CHAPTER ELEVEN

Same Page

TIFFANY

"You look like hell. What have you been doing all day? And why are you not working the store? They're so busy up there. I've been trying to reach you, but you wouldn't answer!" Abbey releases a torrent of questions my way as soon as I open the door.

"Slow down, everything is fine. I've just been... under the weather."

I sit back down onto the couch.

"You know, just when I thought that... this is it. That I found the man of my dreams. That he finally came back into my life. I like him, he likes me. What could go wrong? Life comes swinging at me."

"Oh, no. What did he do? He didn't cheat on you, did he? Did you find out he is married, after all?" she asks me, worry now etched on her face.

"No... Nothing like that. He casually told me that he's only here, in Yellow Point for a year. Actually, even less than a year."

"What? What is that supposed to mean?" Abbey acts just as shocked as I must have been a week ago on that beach.

"I don't know. Something about the project at the school. It finishes when the school year ends so, he has to go back to Newport."

"So, Tyler will leave in June?" she asks me.

"Pretty much. You know, when he told me that I felt so... so stupid. So naive, so... Like I had traveled in time, somehow and was, once again, the student faced with her teacher. I didn't feel at all like a grown adult in charge of her life. And I was so angry..."

"Did you have a big fight?"

"No, not angry like that. Angry at everything. At life, at this stupid situation. It's not fair, you know?"

"Hold on a second!" Abbey says. "Why can't he just stay?"

"The project ends, and the school has no position for him. What is he supposed to do here? Become a fisherman?" I laugh but it's sorrowful and harsh. "He's worked so hard for his career; he has a book coming out..."

"Alright. Then why don't you move to the city with him?"

"That's exactly what Tyler asked me. When I started to get upset, when I accused him of not putting me first, he pointed out this very thing to me. And I realized that, in the same way he can't leave his job in the city, I can't leave the toy store. June left me in charge of it, and I love it."

The immensity of this situation grips me once more. I lie down on the couch and grab one of the pillows for support. Abbey takes my hand and tries to cheer me up.

"No, don't do this. Come on. There has to be a way. We'll find it. Better yet, you and Tyler will find it together!"

"I don't know anymore, Abbey. I sincerely feel as if the world is against me. When Tyler came back into my life, I thought that this was it. I thought it was fate. It would be him and me against the world, filling out the love story that we were not able to live back then."

"Honey... and please don't take it the wrong way when I say this. Is it possible that all this was just... a projection of yours?" Abbey asks me.

"What does that mean?"

"You know... That you used to have a crush on your college teacher. By luck or coincidence or whatever you want to call it, he happened to come and teach here, in Yellow Point. Is it possible that you were simply carrying through a fantasy that you had as a college girl? Think about it. Are you truly in love with Tyler or is he just a projection of your own fantasy?"

I stare into space as my friend's question sinks into my soul. When she notices that I don't answer, Abbey pushes forward.

"Okay... let me ask you something else. Is this in any way related to Brian? And the fact that he cheated on you with that waitress?"

"How could these two things be related?" I ask her.

"Well, it seems to me that, despite you dismissing the idea that you were hurt about Brian's cheating, you... were, in fact affected by it."

"Of course, I was affected by it, Abbey. I'm not made of stone. Brian and I dated for a long time. But it didn't hurt me in the way everyone and now you, seems to think. It took me by surprise but that was it."

"Are you sure?" she asks me. "Because I think that this is something worth exploring. Brian cheated on you, and you dumped him. Then Tyler comes out of nowhere. Your old college professor that you used to have a crush on. And you throw yourself at him, claiming that you two are meant to be..."

"I did not throw myself at him! Oh, my God! Is this what you think about me? Is this what the entire town thinks I did?" I realize as the conversation continues.

"No, no, that's not what I meant. I was speaking... literally? That you threw yourself into this relationship with Tyler. But, perhaps it wasn't out of genuine love. But more so out of lust, based on your past with him and out of hurt because of Brian. Look, Tiff, what I'm trying to say is this. Are you sure you're in love with Tyler? And that you want to pursue this? Because it looks like an awfully complicated relationship."

"I... suppose I never thought about it this way. But the truth is... that I do want to pursue this. I get what you're telling me, Abbey. Tyler is not just a fantasy or an itch that I'm scratching. He has proved to be a wonderful, kind, smart man with whom I could see myself spending the rest of my life with."

She smiles and scratches her forehead, trying to find the next thing to say. Or, perhaps, she already knows what she's going to say but she doesn't know how to say it.

"Umm... Tiffany... Are you sure that Tyler feels the same way about you?"

"Why wouldn't he? Because he wants to go back to the city after his job here is done? That's... just because..." my words get lost.

"Tiff... you need to talk to him. And fast. There is no point in continuing this if he doesn't see things the same way as you."

"Yeah, I guess you're right. I've been cooped up in here and I didn't even think about his feelings. I just focused on myself and how upset I was. But you know what? I'll go down to the school and talk to him."

Abbey gives me an odd look that I can't quite comprehend.

"What? What is it?" I ask her.

"Nothing. I just... Mmm... Nothing. You want to go to the school and see him?"

"Yeah. What's wrong with that?"

"Nothing, I guess..."

***

The Yellow Point school yard is buzzing, filled with students who are chatting, laughing, chasing each other, engaged in different sports or playing games that they invented and for which only they know the rules. I climb the steps and walk inside, the familiar smell of disinfectant and cheap air freshener hitting me like a blast from the past. A group of teachers are huddled in a corner, watching over the children. They see me and wave.

"Hello, Tiffany! Are you here looking for clients, then?"

For a moment, I don't understand what they're talking about.

"What do you mean?"

"Because of the toy store... Do you have something planned for the kids?"

"Ah! No, no. I'm just looking for Tyler. Tyler Stone. Professor Stone, I mean. Do you know where I can find him, by the way?"

"Sure... if he's not in one of the classrooms, he should be in his office. Second floor, third door to the right. You can't miss it."

I nod as a thank you and start to climb the stairs. Even though I refuse to turn my head back around to check, I hear them talking and hope they went back to their previous conversation, not a new one about me and Tyler. I focus on my discussion with Tyler and continue on my way.

After a few knocks on the third door to the right, I hear his tired voice telling me to come in. His face is a combination of shock and disbelief when he sees me walk into his office, not exactly the greeting I was expecting.

"Hi, Tyler! How are you? Sorry for not calling. I just decided to come and talk to you and..."

"Tiffany, what are you doing here?" he asks me and runs a hand through his hair, nervously.

"I... just told you. I decided on the spur of the moment to come and talk to you. And here I am," I smile.

"Don't you think it should probably wait? I'm off in only two hours."

"Umm... I guess it could wait. But I really needed to talk to you. Tyler, I feel bad about the way we left things the other day. When you told me that you are only here in Yellow Point until June or so. And I think that we need to discuss it more. To discuss where we are and how we feel about each other as a couple."

"A couple?"

His question floors me. I feel as if a train has hit me full on, knocking the wind out of me. I grab the wooden armrest of the chair and hold on to it as if for dear life.

"Yes Tyler, a couple. What would you call us?" I ask him.

He starts to play with a mechanical pencil on his desk, obsessively pushing the end in rhythmical clicks. I can tell that he's nervous, but I simply can't understand why.

"Tiffany, look. I don't think that this is a conversation we should be having here. That's all."

"What is that supposed to mean? Why shouldn't we have this conversation here?"

"Because this is a professional environment, Tiffany. It's the school where I work. I don't like the idea of discussing my private life in my office where, at any point, a colleague of mine or, worse, a student, could walk in."

"Tyler, I understand what you're saying. But we're only talking. Nothing else is happening. Even if another teacher or even a student would walk in, we would just be sitting here, separated by a desk, talking. It's as if we're at a bank or something."

"No, that's not at all what's happening, and I don't like the fact that you refuse to be on the same page with me on this one, Tiffany."

"I don't *refuse to be on the same page* with you. I simply disagree. Look, Tyler... Do you not want me here? At the school? Is that what's happening?"

He looks at me with a serious face but maintains his silence, which I interpret as the answer, perhaps even louder than any sentence he could have uttered.

"Oh, wow... That's just... And here I was, running back to you hoping that this was all a misunderstanding. That you would welcome me with open arms, and that we would work on a solution together so that we can be... well, I was going to say a couple. But it seems like even this is news to you. Much like that fact that you don't want people to see me at the school is news to me. Great..."

I pick up my bag off the floor and head out.

"Tiffany, that's not what I said! You're taking everything out of context! I just said that this is not very professional."

"Yeah. That's the point, isn't it? That you care about your job here much more than you care about me. You know what else, Tyler? That's exactly what happened ten years ago. You cared about your job then a lot more then, too! You know very well that you were in love with me. And yet, you did nothing. You let me slip away after that kiss because your job, your precious position meant far more. And here I am, ten years later, just as stupid as I was back then, allowing you to do the same thing to me all over again!"

I walk out of his office and slam the door even though I didn't mean to, drama not being something I tend towards. But I am glad that I got my point across. Still as I walk out of the school, I cannot help but realize one thing. Tyler Stone has not changed at all. He is still the professor, and I am still the young, naive student. I am quite the idiot, aren't I?

Chapter Twelve

Years

Tyler

The door of my office slams hard and makes the paintings on the walls shake. I wish I could stop her but there is hardly any chance of that happening. What can I do? Run down the school halls after my girlfriend like a teenage boy? The students would never respect me again. I tried telling Tiffany that this is not the right place to have this conversation, but she would simply not listen. And now, here we are.

I try to call her, but she refuses to answer. As a result, I leave a series of messages, apologizing and giving my side of the story, more explanations, and other relevant pieces of information that I think would help the situation. They all go unanswered as Tiffany ignores me.

Finally, I get up from my desk and head to the main conference room where I am supposed to attend a meeting with some of the other teachers. I just have no clue how I will be able to focus.

"Hey, Tyler! Was that... Tiffany Hart I saw down the hallway earlier?" another teacher asks me.

"Umm... Yes. Why?"

"No reason, no reason."

They all look at me with a strange gleam in their eyes, and I can tell what they're thinking. But I try to ignore it as Mrs. Walden, the principal, walks in and prepares for the meeting. Sitting at the same oval table as me, two of the younger teachers, both women, have now hidden their mouth behind their hands and are chattering away happily.

Could they be talking about me and Tiffany? The idea is eating at me slowly and I can feel sweat running down my back. I open my leather organizer and scribble something down, looking busy and scribbling something to just focus my eyes. Finally, Mrs. Walden stands up, clears her throat, and starts the meeting.

"Good afternoon! Only a few things on the agenda today, then... I've named Mr. Halston, our lovely gym teacher, in charge of the Halloween festivities."

Everyone around the oval table nods.

"Get ready for the decorations, then. The kids will also most likely show up in costume, they will try to prank each other, like they do each year... So, let's keep an eye on them to make sure that everyone is safe. Alright?"

We all agree.

"Good. Now, we have also received a brand-new set of uniforms for the basketball team, I am proud to say. I am less proud to say that, since they were sponsored by the local pizza place here in Yellow Town, every T-shirt says "Eat at Ray's Pizza, We're Yellow and Mellow!" So, you know, you win some, you lose some."

The teachers around the oval table giggle, and the meeting goes on.

"Tyler," she addresses me all of a sudden, making me jump.

"Yes, Mrs. Walden?"

"You need to organize a parent-teacher conference soon. And by soon, I mean in a week or two. You are a new teacher here and I am sure that the parents have a lot of questions for you or just want to meet you. So, please, make that happen."

"Yes, Mrs. Walden, I will."

"And... Tyler, please don't..."

She stops and stares at me, one of the sidepieces of her large glasses in her mouth.

"Yes, Mrs. Walden?"

"Never mind. Just make the parent teacher conference happen."

"Yes."

Immediately, the two young teachers who were chat chatting earlier go at it again, this time with no shame. Even though I cannot hear them, I am convinced that they are talking about me. I try to act as normal as possible and make a note about the parent-teacher conference in my agenda.

Mrs. Walden resumes her speech about the comings and goings at the school but my mind wanders. I think about Tiffany and her reaction. Does she truly think that I am rejecting her? In fact, does she think that I rejected her back then as well? Because this could not be further from the truth. I am in an impossible position where I have to consider my job.

Above everything else? Tiffany seems to think so. This is something I need to fix and fast, before I lose her. That cannot happen.

"... you listening to me? Tyler, are you here with us?" Mrs. Walden's voice comes as if from a distant planet.

"What? Yes, of course, Mrs. Walden. What were you saying?"

"That we need to start planning the Christmas talent show. I know that it's still a while before Christmas, but the children need to practice. Do you think you could put forward some ideas of plays that the children might love to be a part of this year?" she asks me.

"Absolutely, Mrs. Walden. It would be my pleasure."

"Great. But nothing too... *city*, okay?" she turns to me one more time.

"What... does 'too city' mean?" I ask her.

"Well, you know. We're a small town here, in Yellow Point, and we don't like... weird things. Just make sure it's a nice, traditional play with nothing out of the ordinary going on."

There are several things I would like to answer to the principal, but I understand that it's not a good idea to antagonize this woman. Finally, the meeting has come to an end, and she announces her goodbyes. I get up to leave when I feel a small and bony hand pulling on my sleeve.

"Tyler? I need to see you in my office please," Mrs. Walden says.

My heart sinks to my knees as I realize what she wants to talk to me about.

***

The principal's office smells like rubbing alcohol and licorice, a strange combination, even for her. I get a yearning to ask her about this particular combination of smells and where it could come from, but I refrain from some personal questions. She does no such thing when it comes to me.

"Alright, here's the deal, Tyler," she crosses her hands on top of the desk. "I don't know how things are done at the college, but here, in Yellow Point, we don't do this type of stuff."

"I'm sorry, Mrs. Walden, clearly I've missed something. Can you catch me up?. What... are you talking about?" I ask her.

"You know what I'm talking about, Tyler. And I'm going to be as frank with you as possible. I cannot tell you what to do because I don't have that kind of authority over you, of course. But I will tell you that, in this town, we value decency and tradition above everything else. We are hardworking people and love to raise our kids in the same way."

I stare at her in confusion, still not understanding what she's getting at. I have a slight suspicion that she is referring to Tiffany visiting me at school today. However, at the same time, I feel as if the principal is making far too big of a deal of out of something that barely happened, and I'm left as perplexed as a magician's audience, where logic has disappeared without a trapdoor in sight.

"Mrs. Walden, could you be more specific? I just don't know what you're talking about."

"Tyler, this thing that you have going on with Tiffany Hart is... not going to work," she says bluntly.

"What do you mean... not going to work? For who?"

"You are a teacher at this school," Mrs. Walden says.

"And? Am I not allowed to have people visit me? Is it because we're not married? Come on, you cannot possibly be this arcane!" I start to laugh.

She looks at me sideways.

"Tyler, I don't know if you truly don't understand or you're just pretending not to understand. Perhaps this is something that happens all the time where you're from. But not here. Not Yellow Point."

"What is happening exactly? Mrs. Walden, if you don't speak plainly..." I tell her as I start to get more and more peeved.

"Tiffany," the woman says, "is twenty years younger than you."

And there it is. The age gap that seems to have bothered not just Mrs. Walden, not just the school, but the entire town.

"Ah, I see. Is that what it is, Mrs. Walden?"

"Well, it's not nothing," the woman says. "She is so young, and you are a man approaching your fifties. I'm sure you understand that something like this cannot be accepted or tolerated in Yellow Point."

"Accepted or tolerated? Mrs. Walden, I have a great deal of respect for you, for the school, and for the town. Otherwise, I would have never come here. But this is not the Middle Ages. You cannot possibly be serious when you tell me that an entire town has a problem with a relationship between two adults! Two single adults!"

She stares at me and shrugs as if trying to say that this is out of her hands.

"No, Mrs. Walden, this is insanity. Surely, you must see this."

"What I see, Tyler, is a forty-nine-year-old man who has gravely overstepped the line."

"Overstepped... the line? In what way? Tiffany is twenty-eight, Mrs. Walden, not fifteen. She is single. She's not married, she doesn't have children. This is not an affair... How could I have possibly overstepped the line? And help me understand what part the school has in any of my personal life?"

"You are a teacher at this school, Tyler, and you don't seem to understand how small towns work."

"Clearly!"

"How do you think the parents will feel when they learn about this? And they will, because you and Tiffany Hart are not exactly hiding. She came to school today where you, apparently had a fight, and she left after slamming the door to your office and causing disruption."

I feel as if my head is buzzing. No doubt, several people saw that, and now the word has gone out.

"Mrs. Walden, I agree about the incident today and I take full responsibility for it. Although I had no idea that Tiffany would come, it was irresponsible of me to allow that to happen inside the school. However, I don't see why the parents should have any kind of feelings toward this."

"Really? But their children go here," she tells me.

"So?" I don't understand her answer.

"Tyler," she says, now clearly tired of us going around in circles. "The parents won't like the fact that one of the teachers at the school is dating a woman who is twenty years younger than him."

"Why not? What business is it of theirs?"

"What if you decide to date one of the students next?" she tells me.

My anger starts to bubble inside me.

"Mrs. Walden, that is a very serious accusation you are making. Like I said before, Tiffany is twenty-eight, and nowhere near the age a student at this school is. I do hope that this was just you having misspoken."

She clears her throat and tries to take it all back.

"Yes... yes, well. You get my point. The parents might worry. Plus, what will the university say?"

"The university? You mean North Newport? What do they have to do with all this?"

"Well, how will they feel that while you were working on this project in Yellow Point, you spent your time here dating a woman who is twenty years younger than you?"

Once again, I am shocked at the woman's small mindedness and lack of heart.

"Mrs. Walden, I did not spend my time here dating a younger woman. The fact that I have been seeing Tiffany has in no way affected my performance at the school. How can you even say this? Plus, why would the university be interested in my personal life? Unlike you and everyone else in Yellow Point, it seems, that's not how North Newport operates. The quality of a professor is not judged based on whom he is dating."

She spends the next moments in silence, scanning my face. I think that my last remark might have made an impact on her.

"Maybe they *should* consider it; who you surround yourself with certainly hints at the type of person you are. How else do you determine integrity?"

"What? Is that what you truly believe, Mrs. Walden?"

"Tyler, all I am trying to tell you is to watch out. Why are you jeopardizing your position here and why are you risking the outcome of this project? You know very well that, at the end of the year, you have to be reviewed. Now, what will that review say?"

"Mrs. Walden, are you threatening me? We both know it's you who has to give me that review as the principal."

"I am merely telling you that you need to behave yourself. What happened today after Tiffany Hart's visit cannot repeat itself. And you would do better to reconsider your dating... choices," she says.

"But this is not fair. You cannot and should not allow such personal things to influence your professional review of me as a teacher," I tell her. "This does not matter."

"It does matter if the parents are not satisfied with you, are suspicious of you, or nervous about you being around their own children!" she replies.

"You can't possibly know that is a problem, Mrs. Walden. These are just your suppositions based on what happened today!"

"Well, we'll see then, won't we? We'll see what happens at your parent-teacher conference."

I understand by her tone that this meeting is over, and that I am dismissed. I pick up my things and head out the door, my head still ringing with all the things that I've just heard. Outside, in the silence of the hallway, I try to decide what to do.

My footsteps carry me out, into the chill of the October air. It feels cool and welcoming against my hot skin, burning with anger and frustration. But what is the solution? Is Mrs. Walden, right? Should I keep my head down, focus on the project I came here for, and aim for a good review at the end of the year?

That is and has been my goal for coming here, to Yellow Point. A year teaching in a small town that will count as a year working on my doctoral degree. That will help me get my tenure and publish my book. A bad review from the school principal will hinder my career plans.

I walk along the quiet edge of the hilltop that overlooks the ocean. There is nothing here but the cold wind, the seagulls, and the sound of the icy waves crashing into the dark sand. What a gorgeous and poetic backdrop for my little drama. Who would have known?

In the same way, who would have known that here, of all places, I would find my heart's desire? The one woman that reignited the roaring fire that my heart is evidently capable of?

Chapter Thirteen

Obligations

Tiffany

I can hear the knocking on my door, but I decide to ignore it. It's probably just the delivery driver dropping off my new body lotions and vitamin supplements. My head is too full, and my emotions are in complete disarray. Whoever it is, they can wait. Still, the knocking continues. Not a delivery driver. Frustrated and irritated, I get up from my desk and stomp down the hallway as if to punish it, and open the door.

"Oh, it's you, hi..." I say as I see Tyler standing there, holding a large bouquet of roses and a bottle of wine.

"Who else?" he smiles. "Can I come in?"

"If you want to..."

He makes his way inside and hands me the roses. They smell sweet, almost like honey and jam, reminding me of summer days and happiness.

"Ah thank you Tyler. You didn't have to do this," I tell him.

"I know. But I thought they might brighten your day."

I move into the kitchen to find a vase for the roses and the conversation stalls for a few moments. It becomes slightly awkward, even though there should be so many things to say between us. He's finally here, with me, and although I'm peeved to no end, I'm also exceedingly thankful that he isn't anywhere else at this moment.

"Why are you here, Tyler?" I ask him.

"You haven't been answering my calls or my texts, Tiffany. I started to get worried."

"Did you?"

"Please, don't do that. You know how much I care about you. And you also know that I do worry about your well-being," he replies, the same kindness of always etched in his handsome face.

There is nothing I would love more in this instant than to throw myself in Tyler's arms. To find that happy place once more and simply get lost in his warmth, his scent, the fantasy of him, the fantasy of us being together. But I am afraid that's all it is. A fantasy. And something inside keeps me from him.

"My well-being is intact, Tyler. It's just that, after our last conversations, both at the beach and later and the school, I don't exactly know what to believe anymore. It may not be clear what you want, but it's clear enough what you don't want."

"That's precisely what I came here to talk about. The last two conversations we had were abysmal. They went completely awry, and I think that what we have, what we could be building, merits a closer look. Can we mend this little snag? I'm afraid that certain events and conversations were just misunderstood."

"Were they? Tyler, you told me plain and clear on the beach that you can only stay in Yellow Point until June."

"That's true, Tiffany. But it's also something that is beyond my control. You know this very well... The school doesn't have a position for me after that. I am scheduled to return to Newport. To my job, my career, my book.

Why are you acting like this is not the reality of my life and as if I did this on purpose to hurt you?" he asks me.

I look to the side, getting more and more frustrated by the minute.

"Ok. I have a better question for you, Tyler. If this is, indeed, the situation, then why didn't you tell me all this earlier? Why did you wait until we went on dates, kissed, were...intimate several times to tell me? Why?"

"First of all because I assumed you already knew this was a project. I thought I explained this to you that first night. And second, because I did not think that things between us could possibly be this serious. It was only when I realized that in your presence, I was being lifted off the very ground I stood upon, all bound up by the beating of my own heart, it's vibrations and resonances carrying me further and further away from the inane happenings of daily life, that I thought I should make things clearer," he tries to explain, "for both of us."

Shit. The man does have a way with words. Still, I couldn't give in to those beckoning eyes just yet. "Oh, I see. Is that why, at the school the other day, you told me that you were not aware we were in a couple? Tyler, you're contradicting yourself at a time when consistency of thought matters. Whether you're lying to me or lying to yourself or..."

"No, that's just it. That's the other reason why I came to see you tonight. We need to talk about what happened at the school. Among other things. You... took me by surprise."

"By just showing up? How is that possible?" I start to laugh, not out of humor but from pure nerves and disbelief at what I'm hearing.

"I wasn't expecting you to show up at the school unannounced," he says.

I pace back and forth a little, trying to calm myself.

"Unannounced? Tyler, the other teachers' wives go to the school all the time. To take them their packed lunch, to help clean, decorate for special occasions, for bake sales, to raise funds for the school... how come the other wives get to go to the school whenever they want but when I come simply to talk to you, it's a shock?"

He stares at me and swallows.

"I meant... Well... We're not married, so... Tiffany, look. You know very well how the town of Yellow Point operates. Our relationship does not have the same status as a marriage."

"What is that supposed to mean?" I ask him.

"You know what that means Tiff…"

"No, I don't, Tyler!" I answer, getting more and more upset. "And, anyway, is this what you came to tell me? That our relationship is not the same as a marriage? And that I cannot come to visit you at the school? And that, somehow, this entire situation is my fault? Or… or the town's fault? Come on!"

"Tiffany, again, you're reading this all wrong!" he tries to defend himself.

Ugh. Why are relationships so hard? All I want to do in this moment is talk to my friend June. We've known each other for so long and she's really very good at deciphering boy-talk gobbledy-gook. She's still in Paris though, a universe away. I'm going to wear my big girl pants and do this on my own.

"Am I, though? Because I feel as if, for the first time, possibly since I've met you, I'm reading things clearly, Tyler. Let me tell you what I think is happening. You do not want a relationship with me at all. Not a real one. You want to focus on your career, which is the most important thing in your life, and has always been. As a result, you don't... want anything, including me, to come in your way!"

"That's just not true! That's not it at all!"

"That's exactly what you did back then, Tyler. When I was in college, and we had our first chance. You pushed me away, exactly like you're pushing me away now."

"Tiffany, you know very well that I couldn't pursue our relationship back then. You were my student. Dating you would have been my final act! A career-ending, black-list making, irresponsible and unforgivable decision!" he says. "I never would be able to find work as a professor again!"

"I wasn't your student forever, Tyler. After the year was over, we were free to do whatever we wanted. So? Why didn't you look for me? Call me, text me?" I demand an answer, feeling tears pooling in my eyes.

"Because..."

"Because it would have damaged your image. And your career. To date a student or a girl much younger than you. And that's exactly what's happening now. Wow... I can't believe you're doing this to me all over again, Tyler. You know what hurts the most? The fact that I thought this time would be different. But nothing has changed. Zero."

"Don't say that. You know how I feel about you, Tiffany..."

"Then what?? What is your solution to all this, Tyler? How do you see things between us proceeding?"

He runs a hand through his hair as he ponders my question.

"Come with me. You can get your own apartment, or you can live with me. That's not a problem," he suggests.

"And leave the toy shop? How could I do that? I've worked so hard for this business. And it's so successful," I answer, the prospect alone scaring me.

"Get someone else to manage it. You don't have to leave it entirely or close the toy shop. Since it's so successful, you can hire a manager and coach them from afar. Or, sell your portion back to June and live off the proceeds long enough to get settled, and we can figure out your next best move. Why not ? Why not at least talk to June about it?"

"For the same reason, Tyler. Because I feel it's my business. I invested so much time, effort, and energy into it. How can I just sell it? I'm building something real here Tyler, with June."

He smiles a little. His face looks bitter and disappointed now.

"Hmm... does that mean that you are putting the toy shop, your business before me?" he asks me.

My blood runs cold, and I can feel dread permeating my entire being. This isn't going to work out.

"No... not at all. That's not what I was saying... I only meant that..."

"Well, isn't that exactly what you were accusing me of just a minute ago?"

I pause and look into his face. He doesn't appear malicious or angry to me, as if he's trying to one up me or win this argument in any way. Quite the contrary. Tyler is calm but sad and tired and seems as though he merely wants to prove a point and do it objectively.

"Tyler, there is no way I can leave Yellow Point and the toy store. That doesn't mean that I don't want to be with you or that, for me, you mean less than the business. You are two different things that I cannot compare. Like the whole apples and oranges thing, which is way overused. I mean, there are so many other things one could use to compare to highlight differences, yet we all say 'apples and oranges.' How about pistachios and almonds? Soup and watermelon? Or – " I'm rambling. *Shut up Tiffany* I tell myself.

"Right. I know what you mean. But back to what matters Tiff. That is exactly what I've been trying to tell you all along. Not just now. Ten years ago, as well. Much like you thought that things would be different this time around, I thought so too. I knew very well that, back then you blamed me for not pursuing our... relationship. Even though you were far too young and immature and, most likely, that was the wise thing to do. Not just for me and my career, but for your sake as well. This time around, I thought you would understand. Hold yourself like the professional you are, with class and maturity. Unfortunately, that wasn't the case. You stormed into the school and ended up causing a bit of a scene..."

I feel so guilty listening to his words, so foolish and childish.

"Tyler, I'm... I'm sorry. I didn't think about things from that point of view. When I came to the school, I wasn't doing it so that we can fight."

"I know that. And I didn't come here tonight to have a fight with you, Tiffany," he replies truthfully.

"What happened at the school was that I just... wanted to talk to you and see if we can work things out. I never realized that, perhaps, I should have waited."

"I understand. Here we are, then. We're talking about it now. What's the solution?" he asks me, his face and tone of voice getting more and more tired by the minute.

I look at him but I am lost for ideas.

"I can't just come live with you and leave the toy store. And you can't stay in Yellow Point because of your career at North Newport," I sum up our predicament. "Wow... this is some kind of pickle, isn't it?"

He nods.

"We can always... have a long-distance relationship," Tyler suggests.

"Hmm... How long will that last? Until we get so tired and overwhelmed? Until... life gets in the way? And what if we want more from this relationship? A marriage, children? How will we do that? Will you ever agree to raise a child in Yellow Point, Tyler?"

"Will you ever come to be a wife in the city and raise a child there, Tiffany?" he asks me in return.

There is a feeling of soberness and dejection hanging above the room. It seems as though this conversation has served to bring is both down to earth, away from our lovely fantasy. Away from the possibilities of what we could accomplish together.

"I feel like I've just taken a cold shower. Or like I just fell through the ice, you know? In one of those super cold waters and now I am more awake than ever," I tell him.

"Yes, I know what you mean. Reality can have that effect on you. I feel it too."

He crosses the space between us and takes me in his arms. Weirdly enough, the feeling of warmth and safety is still there, the idea of coming home still envelops me like a cozy blanket. I half expected him to feel foreign or alien after our conversation, but his arms provide the same protection, and I realize that I want him all the same.

"I wish I knew what to do..." I whisper, lifting my head to meet his eyes.

"You and me both. Never, in my wildest dreams did I think I was going to find you here, Tiffany. You of all people... And that it would prove to be this difficult."

"Why does it have to be like this?" I ask and deposit my head on his chest.

"Tiffany, I need you know something. Neither my job nor my career come before you. They do not matter to me more than you, and I am not choosing them over you. That's simply... not true. This is just something... I have to do. Our lives are very different and there are too many obstacles in our way to make this work."

I lift my head and look into his eyes again.

"Could we try, do you think?"

"I think... we would be fooling ourselves. And that in the long run, this would become a struggle. Can I be honest with you, Tiffany?"

"Of course. Please..."

"I fear that, if we did indeed try to make this work, we would end up resenting each other. That you would end up resenting me for forcing you to live in a city away from Yellow Point or... for having to work so much. For having to give up the toy store. There could be a million things."

"I would never do that!" I argue.

He runs the tips of his fingers across my lips, making me shiver.

"Shhh... That's what you say now, but..."

The words are lost as he leans down to kiss me. It's a bittersweet feeling, as I now know that this is not just one kiss in a line of a million that we will be sharing through-out the rest of our lives. Our kisses are numbered now, like precious gemstones or black pearls at the bottom of the ocean.

"So... we only have until the end of June?" I ask him.

There is no answer. He continues to caress my face, to kiss my lips, and to hold me as tightly as possible. Right now, now here, in Tyler's arms, it's difficult to imagine that this will all end in only a few months. That he will be gone, and my house will be empty once more, than his presence will be nothing but a memory.

I hang on to him like a drowning woman, trying to make the best of it.

"Can we pretend we have forever?" I ask Tyler.

"We do have forever. In our hearts, it's forever. That's how I feel about you, Tiffany, and that's how I've always felt. That is why the universe has brought me back to you."

"Then why is the universe taking you away from me?"

His lips lock onto mine, silencing everything, including my heart.

CHAPTER FOURTEEN

Conference

TYLER

The large classroom is slowly but surely filling with parents. They are filing in as they chat with each other, smiling and waving. I'm a little taken aback by the fact that none of them are carrying a tablet, a laptop, or even a note pad for taking notes. Usually, my students or come equipped with such materials as well as large cups of coffee and, sometimes, even electronic cigarettes, that I promptly but kindly ban out of my c l a s s - room.

This afternoon, in Yellow Point, I am once again reminded that I am in a small town. The parents all look as if they're just sitting down to watch a country play, a session of vaudeville, or to hear a speech. None of them seem particularly interested in what's happening but, somehow, I am more nervous than ever.

Outside, the gloomy October afternoon has already settled in, turning the windows dark and announcing yet more rain. I clear my throat as loudly as I can, to signal that I am about to start speaking. The chatter doesn't die down, to my annoyance and stress.

"Hello, ladies and gentlemen. Parents of Yellow Town... Thank you for joining me this afternoon. I have to say, holding a parent-teacher conference is a little... foreign to me. Typically, I teach college students, and we all know they don't want to get their parents involved!"

I expect my audience to laugh at this little joke, but they just look at me with bizarre faces as if they don't understand.

"Alright, then... so, Mrs. Walden, the principal has advised me to organize this meeting. Since I am new to the school and to your children, you probably have a lot of questions for me. So, I'll start off sharing the syllabus that your kids are following, my rules about turning in homework, and how I handle absences. Before getting down to class business though, a little about me. I have loved literature since I was young and as soon as I could read, it was the classics for me – Tom Sawyer, anything by Edgar Allan Poe, A Tale of Two Cities, the list goes on and on. I feel like I was raised by the huge oak tree on our property as much as by my parents – we had a little bench built all the way around that tree and collectively, I must have spent years underneath its branches, both of us growing taller together, both of us reaching out for more in our own way." I check my audience and see smiling, nodding faces. Good sign.

As I move through the agenda, the parents seem engaged, asking pertinent questions, wondering how they can support their student in their learning. We laugh at teenage antics, and it feels they are very comfortable with me. A bit too comfortable I soon realize.

"We've covered a lot tonight, and I appreciate you all coming. Are there any further questions?"

Some stare at me, like a pack of lions stares at a deer. Others are shaking their heads, no questions. Then, slowly, a woman at the back of the class raises her hand and speaks.

"Rumors have circulated suggesting that infidelity may have played a role in ending a marriage for you. Is there any truth to this?"

The question takes me completely by surprise, like a train that came out of nowhere and honked loudly, making me jump.

"What? No... where did you get that... information from? No. I have never been married. Also, when I said questions, I meant questions about this Literature class, the school curriculum, the plan for the children's education, and so on..."

They look at each other, trying to fit as best as possible in the small desks. Someone else raises their hand.

"Yes?"

"Mr. Stone, I have a question that I'd rather not be asking. But I can't leave here without asking it, so please be honest. Did you come here, to Yellow Point, because you're running away from the police?"

Once again, I feel struck as if by lightning.

"Where... are you getting these things from. Of course, not. I'm not running away from anything. As you can imagine, the school does background checks. As does North Newport College, where I usually work. How could I be working for both these institutions and be running from the police at the same time? Wouldn't they pick me up in about three seconds?" I laugh awkwardly, trying to keep things casual.

They seem satisfied with this answer, but now even more hands are reaching for the ceiling. I have a nagging suspicion that none of them are about Literature or about the students, their children.

"Did you have an affair with a student at your college?" a woman dressed in leopard print asks me.

I remain rooted to the spot, staring at her, trying my best not to show any emotion. Anything could and might be interpreted.

"What? Where... I mean... Why would you..."

A million things are running through my head now but, most of all, the kiss I shared with Tiffany all those years ago while she was taking my Literature class at North Newport. But how could they know about this? Did Tiffany tell anyone? Did she tell the entire town?

"That's what we heard..." the woman dressed in leopard print continues. "That you used to go with a young girl at that fancy college of yours. Is that true? Is that why they fired you?"

"They did not fire me, Mrs. Candace. Like I said, you know very well that I am here on a program sponsored by North Newport. How could they fire me and send me here at the same time?"

"Fine. Then, is that why they sent you here? Because you were sleeping with a student? To get rid of you?" she asks me.

I can feel beads of sweat forming on my forehead.

"These questions are completely out of line. Nobody is trying to get rid of me, I assure you. These are all just ridiculous, unfounded rumors that clearly have been making the rounds in town. In fact, I am due to return to North Newport in June, when the school year ends. Now, let's return to the order of business. I thought we should discuss the students' progress when it comes to..."

"Are you sleeping with Tiffany Hart?"

I have no clue who asked that question. But it doesn't even matter. In situations such as this one, a town like Yellow Point moves and breathes like one, like a single entity. The people cease to be individuals and give in to the hive mind. If one of them believes something, it seems they all do. I'm frozen in place, a statue of mind and thoughts, my mind alone racing, trying to process what I've just heard.

"What... did you say?"

"Are you or are you not sleeping with Tiffany Hart? The girl who manages the toy store?"

"Alright... I really think that we have gotten off topic here. I have tried to humor these questions as much as possible. But they are far too personal. I'm afraid I cannot accept them, definitely not in the context of a parent teacher meeting."

"But that's exactly why you should accept them. Because we are parents, and we want to know," another woman says.

"I'm sorry, I don't think I understand. Are you Tiffany's parents? Are you my parents? Then why would it matter that you are parents, justifying these questions?" I reply.

"Because you are sleeping with a girl who is twenty years younger than you, Mr. Stone! And, at the same time, spend all your time with our girls as well!"

There it is. The same idea that Mrs. Walden threw at me not so long ago. At this very moment, I'm surprised to find myself filled with gratitude for Mrs. Walden and her obtuse ideas. It inadvertently prepared me for this very specific nonsense.

"I think we need to make a few things clear. First of all, my personal life, preclude an actual crime or moral offense, should interest no one outside of myself. Second of all, Tiffany Hart is well past the age considered to be a grown woman, of sound mind and agency, way older than all of the students in my classes. She is a woman who is nearly 30 years old and has been in plenty of relationships before. She has a college degree, her own home, and she runs a successful business... she is not a fifteen-year-old girl who needs a note to get out of gym class!"

"But this is our business!" another woman fights back.

"What do you mean?"

"How can you say that your personal life is none of our business, Mr. Stone? You teach our girls! Who is to say that you're not teaching our girls to... to date older men? To accept advances from old men? To..."

"Enough, please! This is getting outlandish, and I literally cannot believe that this what it has all come to. I came here to teach the students of Yellow Point. To offer them advanced classes, and to coach them for college. And this is what I get in return? You think I am now teaching your girls to date older men?" I ask incredulously.

"Isn't that what you taught Tiffany Hart? She was your student in college."

The statement falls on me like a block of stone. I had no idea that the parents or the people in Yellow Stone, for that matter, knew this. I look around the classroom and see their faces, triumphant and smug. What a turn of events. Things were going so well.

"Yes, it is true that Miss Hart was a student of mine, a long time ago, in college. But so were thousands of others. I've been a teacher for the past thirty years, Mrs. Candace. Do you have any idea how many others have taken my class? Are you going to say the same thing about them?"

"I don't know. Are you sleeping with all of them?" the woman asks, her eyes now bulging out of her head like she's a pug.

Before my anger gets the better of me, before I lose my patience and say something I deem wildly inappropriate, even though they are the ones who are disrespectful and are pushing my buttons, I need to end this meeting. I offer them a smile instead of peace.

"Alright, we will end things on that note. It seems you don't have any questions related to the curriculum or the students. As a result, I won't waste any more of your time. I will send you some material via email as well as an update on your student's progress. Thank you so much for coming out this afternoon. Drive safely!"

I turn around and pretend to busy myself on the laptop so that I don't give them another chance to ask more questions. Behind me, I can hear the parents getting up. The noises of metal school chairs scraping against the floor tells me that they have accepted to leave. But there is also a lot of chatter, and I am aware that at least some of it must be about me and what just happened at this parent teacher conference.

Suddenly, I am startled and turn around as I can feel a hand tapping me on the shoulder. As I whisk around, I can see a tall woman in a tight, orange dress smile broadly at me. Her makeup is heavy and somewhat oily under the fluorescent lights of the classroom, but she is not unattractive.

"Can I help you, Mrs..."

"It's *Miss*... Levinson," she smiles. "Yes, what do you know, I never married either! Not because of lack of opportunities, mind you! I just didn't... feel like it!"

"I'm sorry, Miss Levinson, was there something you wanted to talk to me about? Or... do you have a child in one of my classes?"

"Oh, goodness me! I'm being so rude! I'm Ronni Levinson!" she says and extends her hand to shake mine. Or, possibly, for me to kiss her hand, I can't quite tell. Her extremely long nails are painted a cherry red.

"Umm... nice to meet you, Miss Levinson. Can I help you in some way?" I repeat, noticing that the woman is not yet stating why she approached me.

She smiles broadly and runs her hand up and down her body, from her waist down to her thigh, in a very suggestive manner. Obviously, she thinks that she's being flirty or coy, but anyone with eyesight could understand what she's doing. All around us, parents have started to notice this interaction as well.

"Well, I was wondering... Umm... I noticed that my Sarah... You know, my daughter, Sarah, is not doing so well in Literature class. But I would like her to do better. Do you offer... mentorship or tutoring at home, Mr.

Stone?" she asks and lowers her voice while she looks me deep in the eyes.

That is quite literally the last thing I need. After the impression that the entire town of Yellow Point has formed about me, I certainly do not need a single middle-aged mother asking me to come to her house.

"Miss Levinson, I'm afraid I do not offer private instruction. Now, if you'll excuse me..."

"Wait, wait!" she grabs my elbow and links her arm in mine.

The rest of the parents who haven't yet left the classroom are now watching us like they're watching a tennis game.

"Miss Levinson, please..."

"Call me Ronni," she says and continues to paw at me.

"Miss Levinson, I must ask you to let go. I'm sure you agree that this is bordering on being quite inappropriate."

"Inappropriate? Goodness me! Don't be silly, Mr. Stone! Now, how about you come to the house this evening, and I will make my famous tuna casserole just for you? And you can tutor Sarah, of course!" she winks, and then leans her entire body into me as the other parents watch, their eyes bulging.

"No, no. Absolutely not! Like I said, I do not offer private instruction, I'm sorry! And tuna casserole... is not for me," I reply before I can stop myself.

I finally manage to extricate myself from her grasp, rearrange my tie, grab my things off the teacher's desk, and walk out of the classroom. Behind me, I leave much animated conversation, even louder than my teenage students make when they're being unruly.

Walking fast down the corridor, I try to get away as quickly as possible. In the street, evening has fallen fully, the October air chilly and damp. However, I don't care. My head still buzzing after what happened at the parent-teacher meeting, I feel as if I need to cool off and calm down.

I charge down the street but, only after a few steps, I bump into someone who balances themselves and starts to apologize. Heavy things fall from the stranger's arms, and I bend down to pick them up.

"Oh, my God, I'm so sorry!"

"No, I'm so sorry! I wasn't looking... I just bumped into you... I... are you hurt?"

"I'm fine, don't worry. Are you alright?"

I look into her face and freeze, my blood going cold, and not because of the chilly October air.

"You're... Abbey... aren't you? Tiffany's friend."

"Yes," she replies. "And you're Tyler. The famous Tyler Stone. I happened to catch your little performance in there. I came to the school to drop off some books from the library. You really know how to captivate an audience," she says.

I have no idea what her take on all of this is, but I do know one thing. It will all get back to Tiffany before I am able even to catch my breath.

"Abbey... this parent-teacher conference was... they cornered me in there and I just... I'm used to students. College students, not children's parents. They threw a bunch of conspiracy theories at me..."

"No, yeah, I know. I saw."

Her answer is hard to read as is her tone of voice and her face. I hand her back the books that we've just collected from the pavement.

"Thank you. Are you going to see Tiffany tonight?" she asks me.

"I don't know, maybe. Why?"

"No reason," she says, "just curious. Thanks for your help, I really do need to run. I'm hoping to check out a nearby property rumored to be haunted and record a session for my channel."

"Oh! That sounds like a good time!" I say awkwardly. "You don't go alone do you?"

"Nah. My cousin offered to come with me for this one."

We say our goodbyes after this, and I watch her walk away, carrying the heavy books. After a few steps, she turns around and addresses me again.

"Tyler, Tiffany really does care about you. In fact, she's in love with you."

"I know."

"But, she's also one of my best friends."

"Yes, I'm aware."

It remains to be seen what that means.

CHAPTER FIFTEEN

Deception

TIFFANY

A set of boxes lies on the floor of the toy store. Some of them are open while others are still sealed, waiting for my attention. Out of the open ones, pink Barbie dolls dressed in various types of bathing suits poke their heads out, looking out with glossy and unmoving eyes though the plastic wrapping that they live in.

I reach for yet another box and dump its contents on the floor. Next to me, my laptop displaying an endless Excel file with my store's inventory, and a cup of coffee that went stale a long time ago. But I still drink it, the caffeine being the only thing that's still keeping me going this late in the evening and after a long day of work.

In the calm and quiet of the toy store, a tap on the front door makes me jump.

"God, it's you... I thought... never mind."

I rush to unlock the front door and allow Abbey inside. She shakes autumn rain off her coat before coming in and smiles.

"Who did you think it was?"

"No one. What's up? Were we supposed to have dinner or something? I'm so sorry. I totally lost track of time. This inventory is proving to be tricky."

I shrug and sit down on one of the boxes. She takes off her coat and does the same. It's quiet and calm once more as I stare at my sweet friend.

"We didn't have anything planned, don't worry. But we can grab a bite or order something if you want," Abbey says. "I was supposed to go check out another property tonight with my cousin but we got rained out."

"Yeah? That's a bummer. Maybe you guys can check it out tomorrow? If your cousin can't make it, let me know. I can probably work something out. And I love watching you lay down the spookiness for your YouTube channel." I glance at her.

"So... what's up, Abbey? You doing ok? Stop by to help? I have about a million things to be done. I have the Halloween decorations and toys that were just brought in and they're supposed to go into the system, some candy, candles, balloons..."

"No, yeah, I get it. It's just that... Umm..."

"Abbey, come on, what is it?" I ask, my impatience getting the better of me.

"I went up to the school tonight. Mrs. Walden asked me to bring some more copies of those Jane Austen and Emily Bronte novels from the library. On loan, you know, because they don't quite have enough..."

"Yes, and?" I say and start playing with the scotch tape on one of the boxes.

I can tell that she's nervous, for some reason, but I don't understand why.

"Yeah, that's right. Why they needed more books is not important right now. So, as I was saying, I went up to the school tonight. And, as it turns out, Tyler had a parent-teacher conference."

"I know, he told me."

"Oh, did he? Ah…"

"I mean, he told me that he was supposed to have the parent-teacher meeting today. We haven't spoken yet. I don't know how it went," I tell Abbey.

"Well… it didn't go down smoothly. Tiffany, as it turns out, everyone there seemed to be aware that you and Tyler are noodled up. And they ain't likin' it. They're saying things like, 'sounds like she's managing toys during the day and studying classics at night,' and something about *you* teaching *him* all the latest in toy trends."

I listen to her talk and shrug again, which she finds surprising.

"Yeah, I already knew that. I mean… I already that the whole town thinks I'm sleeping with him. Which I am, of course. But they were thinking that long before we even kissed. Brian came to the toy store a while back and told me to my face that he thinks I'm sleeping with Tyler. And then random people started asking me about it… So…"

"But what about… the other thing?" Abbey asks me.

"What? The fact that they don't agree? Because there's such an age difference between us? Abbey, come on. Like I'm going to pay attention to what people say. There's an age difference. So? Brian and I were the same age and he cheated on me with a waitress. There. Also, since when am I supposed to care if my town agrees with my relationships or not? What is this? Some sort of contemporary re-enactment of The Scarlett Letter?" I laugh, but I can see that Abbey is not as amused as I am.

"Okay... if you say so. But you should know that I don't think Tyler is on the same page as you are."

"What do you mean, Abbey?"

"Well... The parent-teacher conference went down pretty badly. From what I saw, the parents were really grilling him, and not about Literature – at least towards the end of the conference. Sure, a lot of those questions were insane. But, at the same time, they also think that, since he's sleeping with you, he might also be teaching the teenage girls to... do the same."

I roll my eyes and kick one of the boxes in frustration.

"Abbey, I get what you're telling me. But this is just... small town mentality. You know, when I hear this stuff, I kind of understand why Tyler doesn't want to live here after his project at the school ends."

"There's something else," she says, looking apprehensive.

"What?"

"When the parents started asking him if he's in a relationship with you, he... didn't say yes. He also didn't defend you or the relationship itself. He kind of just said that you can make your own decisions."

"Abbey... this is just... gossip at this point," I try to waive it all away.

"It's not gossip when I am the one who saw it and am telling you about it. And there's more."

"What now?" I ask, feeling more and more frustrated by the minute.

"At the end of the parent-teacher meeting, Tyler seemed to be...well, Ronni Levinson was touching him in a very...familiar way. They were standing very close to each other and talking."

I stare at her in disbelief, trying to figure out how to react. Or what to feel, for that matter. There is an avalanche of emotions inside me, running wild and causing my head to go dizzy. It's as if I'm suddenly on a roller coaster that has taken a deep plunge and I've just realized that I am not wearing a seat belt.

"Abbey... what are you saying? That Tyler was flirting with another woman?"

"With Ronni to be more precise."

"No, see, now I know you're lying! Ronni... that woman is not even Tyler's type!"

I get up from the box where I had been sitting and pace around a little bit, trying to calm myself down.

"Tiffany? Why would I lie? I'm your best friend. Also, several other people saw it. I came here to tell you tonight because you will hear about it first thing tomorrow. From everyone else. This is going to be the juiciest piece of gossip for weeks to come. I also wanted to be the first to tell you, even before Tyler. Because I didn't want him to lie to you about it."

"Lie to me? What is that supposed to mean?"

"I don't want Tyler to deny it and... fill your head with nonsense," Abbey says.

"You're filling my head with nonsense!" I lash out at her.

"Tiff... all I want is for you to be happy. But this Tyler business is becoming more and more complicated by the minute. First, he can't remain in Yellow Point past June. Which means that your relationship is not even a relationship but... a temporary dalliance, at best. Second, when confronted with the idea, he did not defend your relationship or stand his ground. Third, there's this Ronni

Levinson complication now. Tiffany, I know that you have a soft spot for him because you had a crush on him in college. But how much is too much?"

I feel as if there are a hundred trumpets in my head going off at the same time. I can't think and I don't know what to do anymore.

"This is just... I don't even know if this is true, Abbey! I'm not saying that you're lying to me. But all you saw was him talking to Ronni. That's all. What am I supposed to do now? Dump him based on this?"

"Tiffany, they were not just talking. She was leaning on him, put his arm through his, laughing... You ignored the same type of things about Brian as well."

She utters the last sentence and leaves it hanging in the stale air between us like a bomb. All of a sudden, I am reminded of the experience of my last relationship that ended with Brian, my boyfriend, cheating on me.

"Oh wow, Abbey. Are you actually trying to say that... Tyler is cheating on me in the same way that Brian cheated on me? No... Abbey, Tyler is not the same type of man as Brian. He would never do something like that."

"Tiffany, I am not saying anything. And I am not accusing Tyler of anything without proof. Just like I never accused Brian of anything until we knew for sure that he was sleeping with that waitress. All I'm saying is that it seems to me that Tyler is not on the same page as you."

"Meaning what?" I ask her.

"That you are falling deeper and deeper for him, trying to find a solution so that you two can be together, while this seems to be just a fling for him. A small-town distraction that will keep him busy until he gets back to his real life. And that, perhaps, he has also found another distraction in the shape of Ronni Levinson."

"A distraction? Is that all I am?"

"I just want you to be happy. And not get hurt," she tells me. "I simply don't know how serious Tyler is about all this. Is this how a man who is serious about a relationship acts?"

"Not get hurt. I think it's too late for that."

"Tiff, why don't you talk to him? All I wanted to do is present the facts to you so that you know the whole story and not whatever version he chooses to tell you. But maybe it's time to talk to Tyler about it."

"Yeah, I think you're right. Thanks, Abbey..." I know she has my best interests at heart, but she's always been vulnerable to town gossip too. I don't care about that as much as she does.

She gives me a hug and leaves the toy store; she leaves me to my thoughts and dark ideas. What have I gotten myself into?

***

Late at night, I close the door to the toy store for the final time today and head home. The small streets of Yellow Point are empty and quiet. Somewhere in the distance, the ocean makes its presence known in the sounds of seagulls and salty wind. I can spot the light of a ship somewhere far out on the water, bobbing up and down, like a tiny Christmas light. It's rained and now the streets are muddy, but I brave it all just to get home, my head filled with thoughts about Tyler.

"Well, hello there, stranger!" a whiny voice greets me from somewhere to my right.

I look up startled, and see Ronni Levinson walking her dog, a small pug that snorts and makes pig-like noises constantly. I'm immediately reminded of one night when Abbey and Ethan came over for dinner, and Ethan shared some of his funny theories. In addition to athletes and blue collar workers being more present in their bodies

and therefore enjoying sex more than white collar workers, there was another theory that people choose dogs
that either look or act like them. Dammit. Looking at
Ronni Levinson and her strange little nosy pug with its
mushed-up face darting here and there, I briefly thought,
Holy shit he's on to something with that theory.

"Ronni... what are you doing out here in this cold, at
this time?" I ask her, half thinking that the woman seemed
to be waiting for someone.

"Well, I'm walking the dog, don't you know? My
daughter Sarah, was supposed to. But you know how
these teenagers are. Never get married and have children,
Tiffany, baby. That's a good piece of advice for you!"
she laughs, the high-pitched noised resounding across the
empty street.

"Thanks... Anyway, I have to get home."

"Hey, listen, I hope there's no hard feelings, right?" she
tells me laconically.

"What... do you mean? Hard feelings about what?"

"Tyler."

His name out of her mouth gives me pause, my head
spins, and my fists ball up. The way she pronounces it so

casually, so intimately, as if they have known each other for a century, upset me much more than it should.

"Tyler? What about him?"

"Well, I asked him if he wants to give my Sarah some private lessons for her Literature class. Of course, that's all I meant. Just lessons for my Sarah. He was too sweet and offered to come to the house and... well... I did get the feeling that he was, well, coming on to me."

For a moment, I have a mental image of chasing Ronni Levinson down the street while I throw rotten eggs at her. And her tiny dog.

"Ronni, what are you talking about? Are you trying to tell me that Tyler made a pass at you?"

"Honey, he was all over me! The moment I asked if he would like to tutor my Sarah, I guess he saw it as an invitation. I was against it, of course, because we all know that he's seeing you. But he assured me and everyone else at the parent-teacher conference that it's not the case. As a result..."

"As a result, what?" I ask her through gritted teeth.

"I might just follow through, you know. After all, he's such a handsome and charming man. And a professor at North Newport, no less! Why would I say no? I just wanted to check with you and make sure there are no hard feelings," she smiles saccharine sweetly.

I feel sick to my stomach.

"Ronni, were you waiting for me to tell me all this?" I ask her.

"Goodness, no!" she says, but I can tell that she's lying. The woman is enjoying herself and my own personal torture. "I am just walking the dog and happened to see you out here!"

"Mhm... well, then. Have a great night."

I turn around and walk down the street in the direction of my own house, my feet numb, my brain whirring. She calls out to me.

"Come by for some tea, won't you?"

I have half a mind to turn around and throw an endless river of obscenities and dirty looks her way. It would make me feel better for the time being, but it would only confirm her opinion of me. So, what would be the point? Instead, I keep walking toward my own house.

When I reach the cobbled alley, I turn left and instead of walking up to my own door, I turn to head to Tyler's. The lights are on, and I can see that he is home.

I take a deep breath and knock on his door and wait for him to open.

"Tiffany is everything alright?" he asks me.

CHAPTER SIXTEEN

Absent

TYLER

The banging on my door matches the banging headache that has been throbbing since I got home. I get up from the sofa and open the door. Standing there with a murderous look on her face is Tiffany, ready to throw a storm my way.

"I just have a single question for you, Tyler. Why?"

I sigh. I really was not built for so much drama, and I'm growing exceedingly weary of a single question in reply that seems to have become my own personal mantra or something. *What do you mean?* I can't force myself to ask it one more time. "What's wrong?"

"What's wrong? Wow... You really have some nerve; do you know that? Or do you just think I'm that stupid?" she asks me.

"Please, come inside the house. I'm so looking forward to being comfortable for this little chat."

She agrees to come inside but her attitude does not change, and I can see just how angry she is.

"Tyler, I trusted you!"

"I'm happy to hear that. But I am less happy to hear that you're using the past tense. Why are you no longer trusting me?" I ask as I plop down on the sofa.

"Oh, stop it with the Literature teacher bullshit! I am not one of your students anymore, Tyler! You cannot do this to me. I won't accept it!"

"But I'm not doing anything," I try to defend myself, even though I don't even know what I'm defending myself against. "Tiffany, please tell me why you're mad, and let's talk about it."

"God, you're actually going to do this," she says. "You're going to stand there and pretend like you haven't got a clue what's going on. What an act! What a display, Tyler! Bravo!" she says sarcastically and starts to clap.

"Tiffany... please. You chose to come to my house and start this... fight or discussion or whatever you want to call it. If you're not going to communicate with me directly and calmly, I might add, then there's no point to this."

I can see that my comment does not please her. In fact, it only serves to make her angrier.

"Fine. You want me to talk directly?? Here it is. Let's talk about the parent-teacher meeting, Tyler! Why don't you start?"

"The parent-teacher meeting... Yes. I knew that was going to come up at some point. Tiffany, the parents as well as most people in Yellow Point know that you and I are in a relationship. And they have a very bad opinion of it. Well, they have a bad opinion of me, since I am older than you and I am also a teacher at the school. But I have to say that I don't care about any of that."

"Really?" she laughs, completely taking me by surprise.

"Of course. But you know this, Tiffany."

"Do I? Then why didn't you defend me? Why didn't you defend our relationship?"

"What... do you mean?"

"At the parent-teacher conference. Why didn't you tell everyone exactly what you told me a second ago. That yes, we are dating and that you don't care what their opinion is?"

"I did... in a way. I told the parents that you are an adult woman who is in charge of her own choices."

"That's not the same, Tyler. How is it that you only say this kind of stuff when we're alone? But when you are confronted by other people, you back down? This is not what I need from you, Tyler. And that's not the type of man I thought you were. Look... I thought you were... I thought you would fight for me. For us. Yes, there are a few small minded people in this town. And they take some time to warm up to outsiders. But that's the whole point. This should have been the moment when you stood up and defended us. And told them that you love me and that our relationship is the most important thing for you. But you didn't, did you?"

I take a few steps back as if wanting to pull myself out of the entire conversation.

"Tiffany, I didn't realize that you wanted me to make a public statement about our relationship."

"I didn't. I'm not talking about you standing on a soap box in the public square, Tyler. I'm saying that when people attack us for no reason, you need to show them that they're wrong. You didn't. You were scared that it would affect, yes, once again, your career, your position at the school, at North Newport... All of that became much more important than fighting for our relationship. Because, evidently, this relationship is not important enough to fight for. This is a fling with an ex-student that will end in June. So, why bother?"

She looks so dejected and sad as she says these things that my heart simply aches. I wish I could disabuse her of these notions, but I just don't know how. Everything that has happened has driven such a wedge between us, a wedge that has now turned into a chasm. Can we cross it?

"Tiffany, we talked about this before. And we came to the conclusion that it's just not true. You refuse to leave your toy store but that doesn't mean it's more important than me, right?"

"Sure. But I would have still defended you and our relationship."

"Please, this is just... Tiffany, we're going round in circles at this point," I tell her as I cross my legs and run my hand through my hair. My headache is worse than ever, but I know that this conversation is far from over.

"Fine. Then let's talk about something else," she says, taking me by surprise.

"OK. great. What?"

"Let's talk about Ronni Levinson!"

I stare at her, not understanding what she's getting at.

"Oh, come on! You know who I'm talking about! Ronni Levinson! Sarah's mom. She said you offered to tutor her daughter, Sarah, and that you were flirting with her."

"Tiffany, that's not true! Where are you getting this from?"

"From her! Where else? I met her just a moment ago. She wanted to make sure that I'm ok with you and her dating, since she heard the rumors about us."

I feel like I'm caught in some kind of twilight zone or as if someone is pulling a prank on me.

"Tiffany, no, that's not how that went down. I promise you that the woman is lying. The truth is that she approached me after the parent-teacher conference to ask me if I want to tutor her daughter, and I refused. Not only that, but I walked out on her! I have no idea why she would tell you something like this. Maybe she feels bad because I rejected her."

"Is that so? Because here's something else I found out. According to people who actually saw you with Ronni Levinson, you did not reject her at all. You were very cozy with the woman, in front of everyone, flirting and all. So, which one is it, Tyler?"

My head feels like it's about to explode. I'm trapped in some sort of Stepford Wives alternate universe and my patience has now run out.

"That's it. I'm sorry, but I cannot do this anymore."

"What are you talking about?" she asks me, her eyes wide in astonishment.

"This... this is your opinion of me? You've known me going ten years back. You're supposed to trust me. Moreover, you are always saying that we are in a relationship and that we have to fight for it. Is this how you are fighting for that relationship? For us? By accusing me of flirting with every woman that comes my way? No, I'm sorry."

"I am not accusing you of flirting, Tyler! I am saying that my best friend, no less, has seen you flirt with Ronni Levinson!" she says.

"No. She did not see me flirting with that woman; I know that because it's simply not true that I did. So great, Tiffany, I guess that you choose to believe everyone else over me then. And that's all there is to it. Tiffany, I cannot do this anymore. This is too hard. You are making this far too hard. And it's not supposed to be like this. When I came here and realized that I found you again, do you have any idea how happy I was? As if my dreams have come true. But this has turned into a nightmare. You are constantly accusing me of not putting you first, of not making you my priority, of not abandoning my career of thirty years to move to this beach town and... do what? No. It's not supposed to be like this. Love is not supposed to be like this."

"Oh, really? I guess love includes my boyfriend flirting with Ronni Levinson, too?" she fights back.

"I did not flirt with her... Tiffany, I am very sorry that this is what Abbey and Ronni Levinson herself have told you. But they are lies. And I am also very sorry that you chose to believe those lies rather than trust me and come here to discuss this with me before accusing me."

"Hold on a second! Are you trying to tell me that... you're the one with the right to be upset?" she laughs, not believing what she's hearing.

"Yes. I have the right to be upset as well. And I am. This is not a relationship. This is just a string of constant accusations for me. From you, from your friend from the people in town who think I'm... doing stuff with their daughters, from the principal of the school. I just... can't take it anymore. You were supposed to be on my side. Clearly that was folly."

She pauses and reflects on my words, her face showing pain.

"No, no. Tyler... this is... I am the victim here! You are the one who refuses to commit to me!" she says.

"I never refused, Tiffany. We agreed that this is a complicated situation in which neither of us can just... abandon our lives and be together like we're teenagers in a movie. Why do you keep insisting that I refuse to commit to you? I asked you to come back with me. I asked you to move in to my house with me!" I tell her as my frustration reaches its peak.

"But I can't do that! My toy store..."

"Then how did you get the idea that I don't want to commit to you?"

"Because you didn't defend me, Tyler. Or our relationship."

"We're going in circles now. Tiffany, I know that you're hurt. I know that your ex-boyfriend cheated on you. But it's not fair to let that bad experience influence your opinion of me. You think that just because Brian did that you, all men will do the same. That I will do the same. Because Brian didn't put your first, neither will I. And the complicated relationship between us, our careers, our jobs, the age gap is not helping."

She stares at me, dumb struck, her face stony.

"I am over Brian. He means nothing to me. I never cared that he cheated on me..." she says in whispers that get caught in her throat.

"I'm not sure that's true, Tiffany."

In the silence of the living room, I make the decision that pains my heart above all else. The situation has become far too complicated, and I am beyond tired. I feel as if there is no return from this mess.

"Tiffany, I think it's time for us to say goodbye."

"What?"

"My feelings for you have not changed. You are and always will be the most special woman in my life. My dream, really... But this is... anything but love. This is pain, argument after argument and accusations without end. We're torturing each other in the name of a fantasy. I'm putting a stop to it."

She looks into my eyes, tears welling up. Without saying another word, Tiffany turns around, leaves my house, and slams the door behind her.

***

It's been weeks now, and I haven't even noticed. Time passes like a ghost, leaving no trace behind it, except for the beatings of my own heart, and the incessant thoughts that run through my mind. Autumn continues its relentless dominion over the town, dressing it in fiery shades of red and orange. At its borders, the ocean frets and foams, cold and distant, a salty stretch meant only for ships and seagulls now.

The Halloween celebration at the school is underway. I watch motionless as the children run around dressed in various characters more or less well-known. They are all fueled by gigantic amounts of sugar which makes them restless and difficult to deal with, but I try. At the end of the day, Mrs. Walden calls me into her office.

She's dressed as Glinda, the good witch in The Wizard of Oz, complete with pointy wand made of tinfoil.

"Yes, take a seat, Tyler. I've been meaning to talk to you."

"Sure. What's up?"

"Mhm. It so seems that these past few weeks you've been a little... absent, haven't you?"

"What do you mean?"

"Well, not in the physical sense. You've not missed a single class. But you are not as attentive as you used to be. Some of the children have said that, in class, you give them long reading or writing assignments and that you don't talk as much as you did in the beginning. Is that true?"

"Hmm... I suppose I have been a little out of sorts. But this is a legitimate learning technique. Reading the material and then writing essays on it. And there is nothing wrong with it," I argue.

"Sure. I agree. But the students are not used to it. Tyler, I have to say. Is this in any way related to that whole Tiffany Hart – Ronni Levinson business?"

I groan, both at the fact that she is bringing up my personal life again, and at the fact that now that Ronni Levinson woman is tied to me, seemingly for all eternity.

"Mrs. Walden, I don't see why you or anyone else, for that matter, have to keep bringing my personal life into conversation. This is so... unprofessional."

"It's not unprofessional when it's affecting your performance at the school, Tyler. I didn't call you into my office out of the blue to ask you how your last date went. I'm not a schoolgirl asking for gossip," she reprimands me. "I asked you to come in here because it seems that your business with these women is making the students complain."

"I have no business with these women!" I can hear myself saying and as I do so, I realize that my worst fears have, indeed, come to life.

Getting involved with Tiffany has, indeed, affected my career, which is what I feared from the beginning.

"Really? So, you didn't sleep with Tiffany Hart? You didn't at least flirt with Ronni Levinson and lead her on that you would tutor her daughter and then never show up?" Mrs. Walden asks me.

"No! No, I... God... this was such a mistake. Mrs. Walden, I should have never come here."

"To my office? I called you in here." she says.

"I should have never come to this town, Mrs. Walden."

I get up and head for the door.

"Wait a minute, this conversation is not over!" she calls after me.

But I am beyond the point of caring now. In my office, I gather my things and get ready to leave. Not just the school, not just my job, but the town itself.

CHAPTER SEVENTEEN

Breakdown

TIFFANY

The Barbie dolls are neatly stacked on their shelves, staring at me with their blue painted eyes. In the toy store, a few people wander around, trying to find the right present that would please a little boy or a little girl. Normally, I would engage into conversation with them and try to help but lately I've been feeling tired and just drained. The past events have taken a toll on me, and it shows.

Just when I am about to go into the back for a bottle of water, the door to the toy store opens and yet another one of my current thorns walks through the door. I groan and rub my face with my hands as if to try and make this ugly vision go away. But sadly, he is far too real.

"What do you want, Brian?"

Immediately, the people in the store turn their heads toward us, ready for some more juicy gossip. This act in itself makes me mad. I am so tired of being the town's source of gossip.

"Hold your horses, woman! What's gotten into you? Is it that time of month or something?"

How did I ever date this man?

"What do you want?"

"I'm a customer like everyone else. Why are you treating me like this?" he says.

"You're just a customer now? Who could you be possibly buying toys for?"

"Crystal, of course," he laughs as if this is the most obvious thing in the world and I am the stupid one for not getting it.

"Crystal?"

"My girlfriend!" he says emphatically and points a finger to his temple as if to indicate his brain or, in my case, a lack of. "Well, the toys are not for her, they're for our son."

I stare at him in disbelief, trying to figure out if Brian is joking or not. At the same time, the other people in the store have completely stopped pretending to shop and are now just as invested in this conversation as I am. This will, no doubt, be the next big topic of conversation in Yellow Point in a matter of minutes. Great.

"Brian... If this is your idea of a joke, I'm not in the mood, okay?"

"Why would this be a joke? And not everything is about you, Tiffany. Crystal is pregnant. We're getting the baby room ready," he says and insults me in the process.

"Crystal... the waitress that you cheated on me with is pregnant?" I ask.

"I don't get it. What's so difficult to believe? I thought you had some kind of college degree, Tiffany. You always bragged about it... You'd think that sleeping with that professor might have made you smarter. I guess not," he says.

"Alright. So, you came into my toy store to tell me that your girlfriend is pregnant and to... insult me?"

"No! I came to buy some fucking toys! But you keep making this about you!" he raises his voice, forcing the people in the store to take note of what was happening around them.

"Brian get your toys at Ferg-Mart or go to Frazier or something. I really, *really* need you to forget about me, ok?" I can feel the well of emotion build up in my chest and start to swirl and spiral, taking with it any hope I had of self-control. It was all just too much. I finally start to unleash, feeling as if a dam has broken inside of me and now all my emotions are coming to the surface. "You cheated on me out of nowhere with a woman that meant nothing to you!!! And now she's having your child? I had to stand by and watch you parade around town with her while everyone talked about me for not "knowing" how to keep a man!"

"Well, that's true…" he says stupidly.

"Shut the fuck up!" I lash out like a tiger. "I had to listen to everyone pity me and tell me how alone I must be now that a scum like you has left me. How I'm never going to find someone else. And now… now there is one more humiliation I have to endure? One more slap to the face?? You casually waltzing in here to buy toys from my store for your adultery baby? No thank you!"

He shrugs and pulls up his pants in a casual and infuriating gesture. I don't know if he understands what I'm telling him, but I don't care at this point.

"And you know what's worse, Brian? That because of you, I pushed away the most wonderful thing that has ever happened to me! I pushed away the man of my dreams! Because you cheated on me, because you and everyone else made me feel so bad about myself, I truly lost all my confidence. Not just in myself, but in men as well. I lost confidence in the man that made me happy, safe, and gave me love. I listened to gossip, and I believed it! I believed all the stupid gossip!"

I turn to the other people in the store and address them fiercely, the way I should have done a long time ago. They stare at me, not knowing what to say.

"Yes! I paid attention to the stupid things you all had to say, and I ruined the best thing that has ever happened to me! Can you all just go? Like, now? I don't need sales this much," I say, knowing full well I was being too childish and upset with the wrong people.

They put down the toys and other merchandise they have been holding and leave, still chattering but clearly shaken by what has happened. Brian stares at me with a vacant expression on his face.

"Why are you still here?"

"So... are you going to sell me those toys or not?" he asks me.

"God, I do hope that your son doesn't inherit your intelligence, Brian."

***

I slam the door to the toy store and lock it even though it's the middle of the afternoon and there are plenty more customers to serve. I don't care about any of that now and muse to myself that it's probably time to call in more hourly help. The November air is frosty, and I wrap my warm scarf around my neck as I walk down the street, heading for Tyler's house. I know that gossip will spread like wildfire, and I want to talk to him before that happens.

As I pass by the Yellow Point library, I can see Abbey coming down the stone steps. She's not wearing her coat or hat, and she's waving at me frantically.

"Hey, Tiffany! Stop! Come in here! We need to talk!"

"Not right now, Abbey. Sorry, I have to get home!"

"Tiff! Come on! Come in here for just a minute! Seriously!"

I make an irritated noise to myself but climb the steps of the library, nonetheless. At least it's warm and cozy in her office. She busies herself making me a cup of warm licorice herbal tea and asks, "What the hell is happening?"

"What do you mean?" I ask as if I'm bored out of my mind and have no idea what she's referring to.

"Mrs. Altman came in here a minute ago and told me that you had a breakdown? In the middle of the toy store? Just a few minutes ago? And that you kicked everyone out? Is that true? Are you alright?" she asks me in a worried voice.

I laugh softly. "God... if that's what they think a breakdown is, they're lucky. They've never had a breakdown. Abbey, Brian came into the toy store. His girlfriend is pregnant, and he wanted to buy toys from me. From my store, of all places."

"No! You're joking! He never... The audacity! Oh, I could just wring his neck with my bare hands!"

"That's exactly what I thought. Basically, I lost it. Not in the sense of a breakdown, but I realized then and there that what Brian did to me affected me much more than

I knew. It made me distrust everything and everyone. Including Tyler, unfortunately."

"Really? You figured that out?"

"Yeah… It was kind of like a veil being lifted off my mind. I saw that what Brian did was horrible. And that it did such a number on me that… when Ronni Levinson, for example, lied and said Tyler was interested in her, I immediately believed her. Why wouldn't I have? My ex-boyfriend cheated on me, so why wouldn't Tyler do the same?"

"Tiffany, you shouldn't blame yourself. I saw them being… I don't know… cozy?" Abbey says.

"What you saw was that Ronni Levinson preying on him. I don't blame you, Abbey. You were looking out for me, and, for that, I thank you. But I'm also not blaming myself. This is just how things happened. They were bound to. But I should have known better. Tyler is a much better man than this."

"What about your relationship with him, then?"

"What about it?"

"Well, you're still in the same situation. You can't leave the toy store and Tyler can't abandon his career and move to Yellow Point. Frankly, would he even want to move here after all the nonsense this town has put him through? What are you going to do?"

"Yes, that is something that Tyler and I will have to discuss. You know... I've been thinking about it. Maybe it's time for me to... let go of this."

"To let go of the toy store?"

"I don't know, Abbey... I feel like I'm holding on to something that doesn't mean what I think it means. Perhaps the toy store has been keeping me afloat these years precisely because I had nothing else. My relationship with Brian was clearly never been a strong one. I mean, we had so much fun in the early days but he just never grew up as I did. So, I tried to find solace in my work. My relationship with any man in general has never been ideal... And I think I know why that is."

"Why?" she asks me.

I look at my best friend and smile.

"Tyler, of course. After I fell in love with him in college, I have never been able to get over him. I kept dreaming that someone like him, equal to him will come along and make me happy. No one ever did. Finally, I gave up dreaming and started dating a random guy that was just... okay."

"That was Brian."

"Exactly. As it turns out, Brian was not even that. He wasn't even okay. But my heart was never satisfied. It's tough to explain. Think about it this way. It's as if you've seen heaven for one brief moment when you were very young and then... you had to come back to earth and live the rest of your life. Ever since then, you've been waiting for someone to take you back, but it never happened."

"But Tyler did show up."

"Yes. And I was so happy... Unspeakably happy. I couldn't believe it. I mean, the fact that he moved right next door no less! That would make anyone believe in fate. In divine intervention. Like we were meant to be. And then... I ruined it all. In fact, I let my bad experience with Brian ruin it all. Isn't that funny?"

"You were hurt, Tiffany. It's understandable."

"Perhaps. But it is forgivable?"

"What do you mean?" she asks me.

"Will Tyler be able to forgive me? He is the one who ended things between us. When he did, I was so hurt... so depressed and heartbroken. I was even angry with him. But now I get it. He didn't deserve it."

"Neither did you, Tiffany. If you want my opinion, both you and Tyler made mistakes in this relationship. I think that you were both so taken by surprise by the fact that you found each other again that you simply did not know how to handle it. You were not wrong when you said that Tyler should have defended you or that he should care less about the school, the college in the city or his career, and care more about you."

"Do you think so?"

"Absolutely. Even with a long and brilliant career like his, nothing should matter more than true love, Tiffany. With that, you are perfectly right."

"Perhaps I was. That's why I need to talk to him about all this. If he even agrees to speak to me. I know how tired he is of all this, and I get it. Frankly, I want all this to be over as well. I want for us to find a solution... to be together."

"So, why don't you call him? I'm sure he'll want to talk to you, and you two can have a long chat about it," Abbey tells me.

"Actually, I was just heading over to his house right now. Maybe I should have bought a bottle of wine first. Do you think I should swing by Ferg-Mart first and get some red wine? What? Why are you looking at me like that? Should it be white wine?"

Abbey is staring at me while her eyes are growing wider and wider.

"Oh, God... you don't know..."

"Know what?"

"Umm... Tiffany, Tyler has left Yellow Point. For good, it seems."

"What? What are you talking about? Are you joking?"

"No, of course not. A few students came into the library this morning and told me. They had some essay to do that was assigned by the replacement teacher. I was surprised, and they explained that Tyler has interrupted the program on personal grounds and has returned to North Newport. Apparently, the students are upset. They liked him and they were looking forward to the Christmas play. They were going to do Romeo and Juliet.

My head is swimming, not able to handle all the information that Abbey has just thrown at me. For some reason, I keep getting mental images of our houses, next to each other. Except that now, when I go home, Tyler won't be there. His house is now empty and dark.

I am alone now. Truly and utterly alone. It's over. He's gone. He's *gone*?

"Abbey... this is just... Tyler left? Without telling me?"

"I guess he thought that you were no longer in a relationship, so..." she tries to explain.

"Yes. I guess he was right."

Chapter Eighteen

Quit

Tyler

College students are walking in and out of the old building of North Newport, rushing here and there, holding cups of coffee, laptops, and tablets. A sight that is so familiar to me, and one I have missed. A few of them smile, wave, or greet me. I wave back, delighted to see them, and catch a glimpse of the fast city pace I'd escaped from. I do love this college.

Inside, the building is the same as always, crowded and cold, the black and white tiles welcoming me like an old friend. As I make my way toward my office, I look out the large windows. There is no ocean here, no smell of salt, no sound of the waves throwing themselves at the shore like a lover in her soulmate's arms.

I think about the evening I spent with Tiffany on the beach. Her body, her soft skin, the way she moved, and all the pleasure I felt. A pleasure that, back then, I thought could possibly last forever. That she could be, would have to be, always mine. But with pleasure always comes pain. That blessed night on the beach was also the beginning of the end for us. After that, things were never the same again.

"Hey, Tyler! Back so soon?"

A colleague wakes me up from my reverie. Don Mason, from the linguistics department greets me happily. We walk together toward my office even though I haven't invited him to do so. But I am far too polite to tell him that I am in no mood for company. And that I have no idea when I will ever be in the mood for company again.

"Hi, Don. How are you? How's the family?"

"Oh, doing good, thanks so much! The wife is well, it's her birthday next month. You should come by! And my son is thinking about a college. I keep telling him to come here, to North Newport but he thinks... well... you know, since I teach here..."

"Things might get a little crowded?" I ask as I unlock the door to my office.

A group of students passes us by and greets us. We walk into my office, and I open a window against the stale smell and despite the cold November air.

"Exactly. So, how are things in... Small Point?" he asks me.

"Yellow Point. I... was supposed to... anyway. Things are... to tell you the truth, things are not necessarily what I thought they would be, Don."

"No? How so?" he asks, settling in to one of the large comfy chairs in my office.

"It's a complicated story. I guess... I met someone while I was there. In fact, she was no stranger. I knew her from before, and life, it seems, still had something in store for us." I find myself slowing down to consider the question, and plop down in the chair opposite of Don's.

"Very good, dear fellow! What went wrong, then?"

"Oh you know smaller towns and the associated rumor mill? All these ridiculous, baseless rumors started going around. The town fought us on even exploring the *possi-*

bility of an actual relationship. They just couldn't handle the bit of an age gap between us, as if she was a small child or something. She's 28 years old! Geez."

"Ah... I see," Don says.

"Things became so complicated... I chose to leave."

"What are you talking about? You left the town and your position there?" he asks me.

"Yes."

"Because of some rumor mill? Tyler, you said yourself every town has one, who cares?"

"The situation was complicated."

"My God, man!" Don starts to laugh. "Tell me something, Tyler. This young woman. Do you love her or was she just... meant to serve as company for a short time in your life? Had it run its course?"

There is no doubt in my mind how to answer this question.

"I love her. And I would very much like to believe that she loves me. But like I said. The situation is complicated."

"How so?"

"We haven't been able to find a way to be together. She runs a very successful store that she doesn't want to

abandon or sell so that she can move to the city and continue our relationship. On the other hand, I can't leave
my position here and move to Yellow Point. The school
doesn't have a job for me there. So..."

To my astonishment, Don starts laughing. Not sarcastically, but merrily and with much gusto.

"So what?" he asks me.

"So, there's no solution for us..." I reply, watching him
continue to laugh.

"Tyler, my good man... here is a solution for you. Quit!
Quit this job! Quit this one and the one in Small Point,
and the next one, and all the other ones that come after
that!"

"It's Yellow Point, and what are you talking about?"

"Tyler, you have been a professor for thirty years now.
It's enough! If this woman is truly the one for you, and she
loves you back, what are you waiting for? Do you plan on
dying alone? A very successful, old professor, here, in this
very office while dreaming about the life you could have
had with this woman? No! Enough! Quit, go to Small
Point, marry her, and... be happy!" he laughs.

"But... what about my classes? My book, my tenure?" I
ask.

"What about them? You can't write your book in Small Point? And what about your classes? Give private lesson to anyone who needs them. Open your own school! There are a million things you can do, my good man!"

"It's Yellow Point. Don, what you're saying is just... How can I give up everything that I've worked for in the past thirty years? It feels like a waste."

"Tyler, nothing is a waste. Yes, you have been working as a professor for a couple of decades but you've also reaped the rewards. How many generations of students have you taught? How many hundreds, thousands of young people have learned to love books because of you? How many have become writers, poets... This is your reward! You can relax now. Nothing has been in vain, and it never will be. Tyler, don't miss the chance of a lifetime because you can't let go of the past."

I am transfixed and, at the same time, transformed by what he's telling me. Images of Tiffany play in my mind's eye. She must have found out by now that I left Yellow Point and my position at school. What must she be thinking now?

***

My head still buzzing after the conversation, I climb into an Uber that takes me on a slow ride through the traffic in the city. For the first time ever, I realize something that shocks me. I do not actually miss it.

The noise, the pollution, the gray people hurrying here and there, the foul smells, the dirt and garbage. The small streets of Yellow Point seem like a fantasy to me now, like a scene in a book I used to read to comfort me.

Finally, the taxi reaches my apartment building. I take the elevator and wait for the doors to open when I come to my level. I step out and stop, not able to believe what I'm seeing.

"Surprise..." she says, smiling sweetly.

"What... what are you doing here? Are you alright?" I ask, hurrying to meet her.

"Yes. I came to see you. The school gave me your home address, believe it or not. I just had to tell them that I needed to return some work items to you, and that – I'm rambling aren't I? I should have called, I know that. But, after our last conversation and given the fact that you just left Yellow Point so out of the blue, I figured that you wouldn't even answer me, more than likely" she says.

"Of course, I would have answered you. How could I not?"

"Tyler... Why did you leave? Are you really past the point of no return with us?"

"Oh... Tiffany... It had nothing to do with you. I had a meeting with Mrs. Walden, the principal. She told me that my relationship with you and all the rumors that Ronni Levinson spread around town affected my performance at school. I suppose it did. I felt so dejected, so defeated. I should have never come to Yellow Point at all. That it was all a mess... I wanted to get away. And then..."

"Then what?" she asks me, her eyes glued to my face, her gaze expectant.

"Then, when I was finally back here, I realized how much I miss you. How much I miss Yellow Point. The ocean, the little streets, your laugh, your smell, your body. God... I'm truly unsure about how I can live without you. My days don't make sense without you."

"Oh! Do you know how long I've waited for you to tell me those words, Tyler? Since I was a teenage girl. Do you really think we can make this work?"

"It's definitely worth taking a chance. I realize it now. I know why I haven't been happy all these years. It's because you were not here. Because we did not have our chance. Tiffany, we were meant to take a chance, find forever together, and we missed it. My soul has been empty ever since, and my life has been a wasteland. I threw myself into work and my career, thinking that those were crucial, the most important things in my life. And they were. But only because I had nothing else. Because I did not have you. You were the part of me that was missing and that I was trying to replace."

She looks at me and smiles.

"I know how you feel. I tried to replace you, Tyler. With other relationships, with work, with... everything I could think of. It did not work. My soul ached for you. My body craved you, and my mind was always restless, thinking about that one moment in time when I could have had it all, had I just... asked for it."

"No, you did ask for it, Tiffany. Life got in the way."

"How about we don't let life get in the way this time? Let's not make the same mistake again," she says.

"I agree!"

She takes a few steps toward me and throws herself into my arms. I can feel her body pressed into mine and a complete and utter happiness fills me. We kiss and embrace for moments on end, hungry for each other.

"Come on, let's go inside," I gasp and unlock the door.

We hurry through the door and straight toward my bedroom, hand in hand, not bothering to turn on any of the lights. Once we reach the bed, she takes off her coat and her shoes. The only thing left is a soft, black dress made of wool that clings to her voluptuous figure like a second skin. She caresses my face with her fingers and pulls me toward her mouth for another, all-consuming kiss.

My hands travel down her backside, and I can feel the roundness of her behind, wrapped in the luxurious dress, nothing but a scrap of lace as underwear underneath. More eager than ever, I pull her dress up until my hands feel her soft skin and I cup her sweet cheeks in my hands. She looks directly at me now and, as she does so, unzips my pants and pulls them down until they fall to the floor.

I can feel myself growing harder and harder when she touches me. But it's not only her touch. Tiffany's beautiful body, the erotic sight of the triangle of lace, already damp and dark with arousal, the way the lace pushes into her, they all serve to drive me mad. She slips her tongue into my mouth as she takes my manhood in her hand.

Her fingers are small and delicate, and I am so aroused and hard that she just barely closes her hand around me. Still, she moves her hand up and down, pleasuring me and making me even harder, hungrier in ways I did not know were possible.

In response, I push her gently onto the bed and kneel in front of her. I take off the lace underwear and watch as she spreads her legs right in front of my face, the most spectacular and erotic sight I have ever seen. The petals open and unfold, warm and fragrant, sweet and dripping with juices. She looks and smells incredible, and I cannot wait to have her, completely.

As she leans back onto the bed, I run my tongue from the bottom to the top, licking up all the goodness. She moans and closes her eyes, her hands now on top my head, begging me not to stop. I can feel her hips moving in close rhythm to the licks my tongue is providing, the pleasure now a choreography of the erotic arts. Slowly and patiently, I lick away, providing as much pleasure as I can and as much pleasure as I know she deserves. Her swollen clitoris is begging for attention as well. I gently suck it in, circling it with my tongue, and hear her moan.

The sight of her body, entirely naked and open in front of me, the luscious breasts poking the air with the hard nipples, her pulsating and swollen clitoris asking for me, fill me with a type of desire that I have never felt before, in my entire life. It is hunger mixed with love and passion. I'm an animal now and this is my dark desire.

I want to slip inside her until she's mine, all mine, and nothing else remains. I get up, and watch as she opens her eyes and looks directly at me. Her bedroom eyes are a thing of wonder, a vision that painters should have immortalized on their canvases. The lust in her eyes pulls me in and I push my hard and thick shaft against her opening. I hear her moan, primal and very deep, asking for me.

I direct the length inside her, inch by inch, satisfying both our wants, our needs. She gasps for air, taking in as much as she can, and I can feel her pulsating around me now. Her legs wrap around me, she lifts her hips a little off the bed to meet me better, and her willing opening takes me inside. All of me.

It's slow at first, as she makes room for my length. But her juices lubricate every single thrust, and her arms hold on to my frame like she's drowning. From above, I watch her beautiful face relax more and more and, with her eyes closed, she relaxes as she enjoys this ride of pure pleasure. A moment later, with her arms outstretched and her legs squeezing me tight, she pulls me in even more, and now I am lost inside her, to my core, ready to burst.

Just the sight of her body moving under me like that, her incredible smell, the smell of a woman enjoying her man, her flower dripping wet all the way to the sheets below are more than enough to drive me insane. I have never felt this close to anyone else before. I don't think I ever will again. Just like me, she is close to her own orgasm now. I can feel it on her, I can see her petals and clitoris swelling, I watch her eyes close tightly.

We let go at the same time and lose ourselves in supreme feelings. Her mouth is open, she pants and moans. Never has a woman been sexier than in these moments. I think I can hear her yell out in pleasure, but I can't quite tell, my own pleasure far too much to bear. We collapse on the bed, next to each other, spent and exhausted, feeling the very last tremors move through our bodies.

I hold her tight, tighter than ever, while she whispers love into my ear.

CHAPTER NINETEEN

Festival

TIFFANY

The ocean frets and foams, stirred by the late December wind. He parks the car in front of my house, and we descend, happy to be back to Yellow Point after almost two months, but at the same time, a little worried about being in town again. From afar, we can hear that the Christmas celebrations are now in full swing.

Tyler wraps an arm around me and kisses my cheek.

"What do you think? Shall we go and have a look, or should we just go home and..." he asks me, eyebrows dancing mischievously.

"Hmmm... I would love to go home and... We haven't done that since, let me think. Oh – wasn't it this morning?" I joke, making him laugh.

"Wow. Has it been that long? God, I even forgot how it feels or how you look completely nude. We need to remedy that instantly. It's been way too long," he keeps up the flirty banter.

"Agreed. But I think we should swing by the town square first. Let's see how things are going."

"Are you sure?" he asks me.

"Yes. We're going to have to face them all anyway, at some point. I think it's better that we get it over with."

"You're the boss!" Tyler says and takes my hand.

We walk down the frozen street toward the town square, the Christmas music becoming louder as we do. The smell of candied apples and caramel popcorn greets us as we approach, piquing my senses and making me hungry, despite the fact that this is precisely what we've been doing in the past two months. Eating and making love. I don't think I could ever get enough, though.

In the main square, a full celebration is on display. The giant inflatable Santa Claus gently swaying back and forth has been put up next to an even bigger Christmas tree, responsible for an incredible aroma of dark and deep forests, of resin and pine. It mixes with the salt in the air, creating a scent of home. I breathe in heavily and hungrily, looking up at Tyler. He's smiling.

"What do you think?" he asks me.

"I think we're home!"

Dozens of wooden stalls have been installed everywhere around the town square. The people of Yellow Point as well as others from towns nearby are offering handcrafted holiday foods, hot sauces, delicate Christmas decorations, handmade sweaters and scarfs and even dog treats in the shape of snowflakes.

Somewhere along the right-hand side, a stall is missing. I imagine it set up but sitting empty and in total darkness, like a rotten tooth among all the others.

"That's where my stall was supposed to be. Usually, I sell Christmas toys every year in that very place," I explain to Tyler as we move along the stalls in search for some mulled wine to warm ourselves up.

"Oh, I see."

"Yeah. But this year I was a little busy with… something else," I grin and look up at his handsome face.

"Do you mean me?" he smiles.

"Oh yes, I mean you."

"I thought you liked it!"

"I loved it! It was much better than sitting in that cold stall and freezing to death, hoping that someone is going to buy a doll or a stuffed dog last minute before Christmas morning!" I explain.

"Well, I'm glad to hear it, sweetheart."

We make our way to the mulled wine stall and order two cups.

"Ah, Tiffany! It's you! I thought you left town!" Mrs. Whitaker tells me. I suspect that she's had some of the mulled wine herself, judging by the color of her cheeks and the slurring of her speech.

"No, Mrs. Whitaker. I just needed a little break, that's all."

"A little break? You were gone for two months! And so were you, Professor Stone! The kids up at the school were going nuts! They really love you up there!"

Tyler looks at her, eyebrows furrowed, as if he was trying to solve a great mystery.

"Umm... I'm glad to hear that, Mrs. Whitaker," he says.

We take the two cups of mulled wine and make our way forward.

"Did you hear that? The kids love me and miss me," he grins.

"Why are you so shocked? I loved you when I was your student," I joke.

"Not like that!" he laughs. "I guess I'm surprised because the kids never gave me any indication that they were so into my classes."

"Don't be modest, Tyler."

"I'm not, I'm just..."

His sentence is interrupted by Abbey, who comes out from the crowd and crashes into me, hugging me tightly.

"Oh – my – God! I missed you so much! How could you just leave for two months?? You have no idea what's been happening around here since you left!" she says, her breath a white mist in the frigid air.

"Hey, Abbey! I missed you too! Slow down girl, you almost knocked my drink right out of my hands!" I reply, laughing.

"Sorry. Hi, Tyler! How are you?"

"Hi, Abbey. I'm fine. And you?" he answers politely.

Since I've told Tyler about the conversation between Abbey and me about him and Ronni, I have always had the impression that he has soured a little on her. Not that he doesn't like her that much but just that he's more cautious around her.

"I'm good, thanks. So, look, this place has been going nuts since you two left!" she says.

"What are you talking about?" I start to laugh. "Who would care that we left?"

"Everyone! First of all, no one thought that Tyler would leave his position at the school. The kids actually really liked you, Tyler, and they were very super bummed out when you left them out of the blue. Plus, their replacement teacher is a crazy loon, so..."

"Yes, I've heard," Tyler says. "It would have been nice to know while I was there, though. Maybe I would not have left in the first place."

"Hold on a second. You truly didn't know?" I ask him.

"No. Not a clue. Look, all my interactions were with Mrs. Walden and with the parents at that awful parent-teacher conference. Mrs. Walden kept telling me how problematic my personal life was and how my decisions were a reflection on the school itself. She all but threatened that if I continue to see little baby Tiffany here, she would be forced to give me a bad review at the end of the school year, which of course would affect my status with North Newport. And then... there was that parent-teacher conference at the end of which the parents bombarded me with idiotic questions and conspiracy theories."

"And afterwards, that Ronni Levinson character hit on you..." I add, still feeling bitter about the whole thing.

Tyler puts an arm around me and kisses me.

"Anyway..."

"Yes, so as I was saying, I never knew that the students liked anything about the classes," Tyler goes on.

"Well, they do. And they were bummed out when you left so all of a sudden. Plus, many of them are saying that they would have loved to have heard more about college and what it takes to get in and succeed," Abbey explains.

"Wow... maybe should see what we can do about that," he replies.

"And then there's you, Miss Fancy Toy Store," Abbey tells me.

"What about me??"

"What do you mean? You left Yellow Point right before Christmas! People went insane! They had no clue what to do for presents or for toys! Your temp worker was sweet, but she did not really have the knowledge of what toys are appropriate for what interests and ages. They were really upset that you weren't around to help."

"You cannot be serious, Abbey!" I say in shock.

"Yup. I think people realized how important the toy store, with you running it, is for the town. Before, I think they kind of took you for granted, you know. A daughter of Yellow Point and someone who will always be here, no matter what. But now they've seen that they treated both you and Tyler badly with all the gossip, rumors, and insinuations. The attitude around here has kind of changed."

"I'm very glad to hear that. I was sort of wondering why no one was giving us evil looks when we walked into the town square holding hands. Maybe that's it," I reply.

"Yes, that will be it. But also... the other thing," Abbey says laconically.

"What other thing?" both Tyler and I ask at the same time.

"Ummm... Brian and his girlfriend, Crystal. As it turns out, Brian dumped her," Abbey says.

"But she's pregnant! With his baby!" I squeal in shock.

"Yes, I know. She still has a few months to go. I think as the idea of having a child sort of settled in, he got spooked.

He's the same old immature man-child we know and love to hate. But there's something else as well."

"More? How much more could there be?" I ask Abbey.

"Well, as it turns out, Brian cheated on her just like he cheated on you. He cheated on her with... Ronni Levinson."

"Shut the hell up! No! Brian and Ronni Levinson?" I cover my mouth with my hand and stare at Abbey, not able to believe the news that she has just delivered. Tyler, on the other hand is smiling.

"Why are you smiling like that? It's not funny, Tyler."

"No, I know. I'm not smiling at the humor of the situation because there is none. I'm very sorry for that Crystal lady. She is pregnant, after all. As I am very sorry for you, Tiffany. Neither of you deserved to be involved with such a character as this Brian individual. But I am pleased because this proves that I had nothing to do with Ronni Levinson. She came on to me, and I said no. As a revenge, I guess, she lied to you, Tiffany."

"Brian definitely said yes," Abbey smirks.

"What a piece of..." I stop myself before uttering more profanities.

"Ok, you know what? Enough gossip. And enough about this Brian business. I just wanted to let you guys know what has happened. And to tell you that because of this nonsense, people have completely changed its opinion on you and your relationship. I guess they realized that Brian is, indeed, foul and that, even though there is an age gap between you two, Tyler is a good man."

"Wow... it took them that long to figure it out?" Tyler says sarcastically.

"I wouldn't complain if I were you. It's a small town, after all. The people here are kind and honest, but very traditional. Give them a little while and they will come around," Abbey says wisely.

"More than a little while. Luckily, we have all the time in the world," Tyler replies and looks at me lovingly.

"So, what are your plans now, guys?" Abbey asks.

"Well, since the toy store has been so sorely missed, I will get back to it. I have some ideas for branching out into kids' birthday parties. And I may look into expanding the store to include book and video sales. I think that Yellow Point will like that," I reply. "And Tyler and I talked about him hosting story time for various age groups, you know to get them interested in literature. I will expand the few books shelves I have in order to make room for age-appropriate classics."

"Age appropriate classics, eh?" Abbey responds. "Give me an example."

"Oh you don't think I know books as well as you, eh?" Tyler responds. "You're probably right, but I do know some things. For starters, I'm a big fan of Roald Dahl. His whimsical stories are a joy to read, and they've been inspiring kids for generations. Dahl is fantastic for young readers; one of the greatest storytellers for children in the 20th century. Every heard of Charlie and the Chocolate Factory? James and the Giant Peach? That's him. It's incredible how books can shape a child's imagination," Tyler responds enthusiastically.

Abbey nods, the corners of her mouth turned down as if she's duly impressed.

Tyler puts his arms around me.

"An expansion sounds like a wonderful plan, sweetheart. If there's anyone who make it work, it's you!"

"What about you, Tyler? What are you planning on doing? Will you stay in Yellow Point or are you going back to Newport after the holidays?"

He looks into my eyes and smiles.

"Back to the city? What for? I'm already home... Everything I need is right here, in front of me, in my arms."

His lips brush against mine and, despite the cold, I can feel the warmth of his love course through me. Close by, a group of children has started to sing Christmas carols. Silent Night plays softly across the frozen air as the lights on the gigantic Christmas tree sparkle brightly.

For the first time in years, I feel happiness, deep and completely, such as I never thought I would.

"Can I tell you a secret?" I ask him in a whisper.

"Of course. You can tell me anything," Tyler replies.

"Back then, in college when I was a student and you were my Literature professor, I had some many dreams, so many fantasies. They all involved you, of course. I dreamed about you day and night, with my eyes open and with my eyes closed. Everywhere I walked, I would see you... I used to imagine what our life together would be like. And you know what? Reality has proved to be better than any dream. This, right now, the life that we have built with each other is far better than anything that I could have imagined. Thank you..."

His hands caress my face, making me feel loved and protected.

"Don't say thank you. Ever. I am the one who should be grateful. Grateful that you chose me, Tiffany. You are incredible. I know that you fell in love with me, that you fell in love with your professor but, the truth is that it was you who taught me so many things. It is because of our time together that I learned what I want, and what I need. I learned who I am. That is all thanks to you. Look at me! Look at my life! I would never have any of this if it hadn't been for you. I would just be a lonely classroom dweller, endlessly working on his book in a dusty office. But now..."

He leans down and kisses me, passionately and hungrily. Snowflakes are falling now, covering Yellow Point in a blanket of white and calm. Caught in a perfect moment, I find myself wishing that time could stand still, that I could be in this instant forever. This happy and this satisfied for the rest of my life.

Epilogue

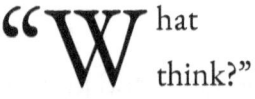

"What do you think?"

"Let's go inside and see what it looks like," I tell her, even though I can already see how excited she is about the house.

To be honest, I am just as excited as Tiffany is, even though I do want to make sure that the house has all the space we need. From the outside, the old house looks perfect. The white and blue exterior makes it picture perfect. When the summer sun shines on it, lighting up its dark roof, I feel like I'm looking at a postcard. Behind it, only a few hundred feet away, the ocean is warming up lazily to the June atmosphere. It already smells of endless vacations and fun.

"Good morning and welcome! It's so nice to see you!"

The Realtor greets us happily. She is extra nice to us, probably because she already knows just how much we love this house and that we are just about ready to do anything to have it.

"Good morning, Diane! So nice to see you again! Do you have a good one for us today? Because that last one was..." Tiffany says.

"I sure do. You've already seen the pictures so, it's time to go inside!"

"Yes, but I'm afraid we don't have a lot of time! Today is..."

"I know, I know. Professor Stone is opening his super elite top notch school today. Yes, the whole town knows and the whole town will be there this afternoon. Don't worry, you two, I won't keep you long. Let's just have a look and you can tell me how you feel about the house!"

Tiffany smiles at me, and we make our way in, following Diane's lead. Tiffany looks exquisite in a dark red dress that complements her perfectly. I watch as she climbs the stairs, her high heels clicking poetically on the old stone steps, her hair bouncing silkily on her shoulders. We've just gotten out of bed, but I long to touch her, to kiss every inch of her skin.

Sometimes I muse to myself how I have become so infatuated with this woman. I love her, of course, but this is more than love. This is adoration. It's the feeling that every bit of me wants to feel her at every moment. And now, as I watch walk inside the house that is meant to be ours, our first home together, my heart soars. How did I ever become so lucky?

"Oh, wow! This is... beautiful!" I hear Tiffany say.

I look around at the large sitting space. The floor to ceiling windows show a view of the garden and, beyond it, the calm ocean. Sunlight is pouring into the large room, and I can just imagine our children playing in here, running in and out from the garden, announcing some new shell they've discovered on the beach while we watch and laugh, happy and satisfied. I never knew that life could be like this.

I muse away while Tiffany checks out the rest of the space on the ground floor. And adjacent dining room, the kitchen, storage spaces and more.

"Are you ready to see the upstairs?"

We both agree and start climbing the stairs.

"What do you think so far?" Tiffany asks me quietly.

"You know the deal. I like it if you like it," I smile.

"Come on, tell me what you really think."

"That is what I really think, though. What's not to like? It's an old and charming house on the beach. It has a huge garden, gigantic windows and... oh... what's the other thing that it has? Oh, yes. You! Preferably naked and preferably all the time!"

"All the time?" she turns around and kisses me, her arms now around my neck.

Because we are on the stairs, we are at the same level. My hands travel down her back, across the satin of the dark red dress, awaking new desires in me, even though I thought they had been satiated just that morning. I had thought wrong. I don't think I could ever get enough of her body and the pleasure it gives me.

"Mhm..." Diane, the Realtor, clears her throat from somewhere at the top of the stairs. "Shall we... go on?"

"Yes, yes, of course."

Tiffany rearranges her dress, and continues climbing the stairs, a little embarrassed but pleased, nonetheless. We have long understood that a passion like our, which started a long time ago and which was forbidden, should not and cannot be contained. Perhaps that is the very reason why we still feel so much desire for each other, the type of desire that manifests itself all the time, with nothing able to contain it. Precisely because, in the beginning, we were not allowed to be together. Now, when we are free, the desire has become all consuming.

"Look at that, our first kiss in our first home together," I whisper to her as we reach the landing of the first floor.

But the tour of the house must continue.

"How many rooms are on this floor?" Tiffany asks the Realtor.

"There are four rooms on the first floor and three more on the second floor. Plus, an attic," she replies. "This means you can easily turn at least two of these bedrooms into nurseries, and one of them into a guest room. The fourth and biggest one will, of course, be your bedroom.

The woman opens a blue door and shows us what would be our bedroom. It's a spacious room with an incredible view overlooking the ocean. On a sunny and lazy day such as this one, the water is calm, painted in shades of turquoise green and gold. Barely a wave can be seen moving.

I imagine Tiffany and myself spending endless nights and mornings in here, our happiness perfect and finally complete.

"What do you think, darling?" I ask her, wrapping my arms around her waist. She looks into my eyes, almost purring like a cat that's being cuddled. Just by the look on her face, I can already tell how much she likes and that she, just like myself is probably imagining our life together in this bedroom, in this house.

"I... love it! This is exactly what I've been dreaming of my entire life," she whispers and kisses me.

"Really? Because you are exactly what I've been dreaming of my entire life," I whisper back.

She giggles and allows me to kiss her face and her neck to my full desire, even though we know that Diane is still in the room. The woman pretends to look out the window at the view of the ocean for a few moments, giving us a little privacy. Finally, she addresses us again.

"The rooms on the second floor... You can turn those into offices if you want. I know that Tiffany is very busy with the toy store now that she's expanding it, isn't that true, Tiffany?"

"Oh, yes. Since I decided to add another level, things have been hectic. I could definitely use a home office. Somewhere I can plan in peace, make orders, answer emails..."

"And you're hiring even more help with the store? Have you figured that out yet?" Diane asks.

"Kind of. I have a few people lined up. I'm supposed to hold some interviews in the following weeks. I'm quite excited, you know?" she squeals.

"As you should be! And you, Tyler?" Diane asks me.

"Well, I'm excited for Tiffany as well. But I have to say, the idea of a home office sounds amazing to me as well. It would surely give me the chance to work on my book in peace and finally be able to finish it. Just imagine... writing in a little nook that overlooks the ocean. Wouldn't that be a dream?"

"It doesn't have to be a dream. With this house, you can have it. But what about the school?"

"It's May now so the school year is almost finished. The school here in Yellow Point has invited me to stay for another year but... I decided to go a different way. As you may know," I cannot help but smile.

"Yes, Tyler is opening his academy for tutoring children and providing college preparatory services. How wonderful is that?" Tiffany says. I can hear the pride in her voice, and it makes me soar.

"That is incredible, I have to say," Diane replies. "And we're all so happy to have you both here in Yellow Point. Then I really won't keep you any longer. How do you feel about the house?"

Tiffany looks up at me.

"What do you think, Tyler? Is this our home?"

"I think so... What about you?"

"I agree. I think we finally found our place."

***

At the bottom of the small hill on which my school is located, it seems as though the entire town of Yellow Point has gathered. There is a lot of noise coming from this merry crowd, but also firecrackers, colorful flags and banners, and even people selling soda and popcorn. Tiffany and I approach and, as soon as people spot us, they start to cheer.

"Calm down, everyone, calm down!" Mrs. Walden calls from the podium where she is presiding over the gathering. "Allow me to say a few words before I let Professor Stone take the stage and tell us all about it!"

The crowd cheers for her, as usual, and she tries to quiet them.

"We owe a big thank you to Professor Stone! His dedication to educating the children of Yellow Point and to ensuring that they have a fighting chance in the race for a good college spot is unmatched! Now, hear me when I say he came to Yellow Point a year ago and we may have seen him as more of an outsider."

Voices from the crowd seem to agree with her.

"And perhaps we were protective of our Tiffany. Or perhaps some of us might have judged Professor Stone too fast and too harshly. Boy, were we wrong! As it turns out, Tyler and Tiffany are two proud citizens of Yellow Point without whom the town could not possibly not be the same!"

More cheers from the crowd. I feel a few hands reaching out and clapping me on the back as if I am a horse that has just won an important sum of money at the races.

"Now, here we stand on the threshold of the new Seaside Success Academy for children of all ages. And we have

Professor Stone to thank! Let's hear a round of applause for him. And then, let's hear from the man himself!"

Mrs. Walden gives me this mighty introduction and calls me onto the stage as the crowd lets out a thunderous applause.

"Yes... Thank you so much. I have to say, I'm so pleased to see so much enthusiasm for learning! First of all, let me say another thank you to Mrs. Walden. We might have had our differences in the past but that all worked out fine in the end! Today, here we stand here as advocates of the children of Yellow Point and surrounding areas, ready to face a new challenge. Please allow me to tell you a few words about the new Seaside Success Academy. When I quit my position at the North Newport College, I wondered what I should do. I was told that I have worked hard enough in my life, made 'enough' of a difference that I should just focus on me, on what I wanted to do with my days. And while my friends and colleagues only want what's best for me, I also knew that I had many more years of service, of teaching in me. What's is better than opening minds to new possibilities, after all?"

Next to the stage, I can see Tiffany, tears now in her eyes.

"As a result, I thought about building the tutoring and college prep services. For young men and women who want to learn, and who need help. I am here to give them that help!"

The crowd erupts into cheer, and I feel like my own heart is going to burst out of my chest.

"I would not however, be here before you today, undertaking such an exciting new endeavor, had it not been for one Tiffany Hart. We figure that between her being in charge of children's play and free imagination through the toy store and me leading on more academic endeavors, we offer between us the perfect balance. This balance between work and play will enable children to truly thrive as they grow up in Yellow Point!"

The people hoot and cheer, happy to see such a display of love. I turn to Tiffany and look down from the height of the stage. Her face is elated but full of emotions at the same time.

"Isn't that something? We are like a yin and yang. So I say now before you all, Tiffany... you are my soul mate. The one person that has been destined for me. There is no doubt about that. I owe all of this to you. My happiness, the incredible life that I get to experience here in Yellow

Point with all of these fine people...all my dreams are coming true. I love you more than anything and anyone in this world."

I reach inside the pocket of my coat and pull out a small velvet box. I can hear the crowd gasping as they understand what's about to happen, but I only have eyes for Tiffany now. Slowly, I get down on one knee and look her in the eyes.

"Tiffany Hart, will you do me the immense honor of being my wife?"

The diamond shines madly in the June sun, casting shards of light like crystalline spears. Tiffany climbs the little wooden stairs and joins me on stage, her face flushed.

"Tyler... when you came to Yellow Point, I thought that all my dreams could now come true. When you told me that you could only stay until June, my heart broke inside me. And now, here we are. June has arrived, and you are asking me to marry you, to build a life together here in Yellow Point. I feel like this has been an incredible adventure that has ended in the most beautiful way possible. Yes, yes, I will marry you. Yes!"

I slip the ring onto her finger, and then scoop her into my arms, beyond happy and fulfilled. The crowd claps, thrilled for our union. In this singular moment, I recognize that this is what my entire life has been building to. So, I stay in this moment and try to make it stretch, to make it count. Make it as happy as can be, recognize it for what it is – paradise.

Also By Rosie Darden

Did you like this book? I'd thank you profusely for leaving an Amazon and/or Goodreads review ! You'll LOVE the other books in the Yellow Point series:

Taking Risks

Taking Refuge

Taking Liberties

Taking Forever